W9-BAY-111

Pokémon™

Pokémon™ SCARLET

HANDBOOK

Stats and facts on 400 Pokémon in the Paldea region!

Pokémon™ VIOLET

SCHOLASTIC INC.

All rights reserved. Published by Scholastic Inc., *Publishers since 1920.* SCHOLASTIC and associated logos are trademarks and/or registered trademarks of Scholastic Inc.

The publisher does not have any control over and does not assume any responsibility for author or third-party websites or their content.

This book is a work of fiction. Names, characters, places, and incidents are either the product of the author's imagination or are used fictitiously, and any resemblance to actual persons, living or dead, business establishments, events, or locales is entirely coincidental.

ISBN 978-1-338-87137-1

10 9 8 7 6 5 4 3   23 24 25 27 28

Printed in the U.S.A. 40
First printing 2023
Cover designed by Cheung Tai. Interior designed by Kay Petronio.

Stock photos © Shutterstock.com

CONTENTS

MEET THE PALDEA POKÉMON!

Welcome to the Paldea region!

There's so much to explore in this exciting new region! You'll meet tons of new Pokémon, find new forms of Pokémon you've encountered before, and learn about new skills many familiar Pokémon have developed.

Pokémon play a huge role in the Paldea region, and Pokémon battles are very popular. The key to success with Pokémon is staying informed. Information about each Pokémon's type, height, weight, and more can make all the difference in raising, battling, and evolving your Pokémon.

In this book, you'll get all the stats and facts you need about the Pokémon of Paldea. You'll find out how each Pokémon evolves, what its Ability is, and what its weaknesses are.

Collect and train as many Pokémon as you can!

You'll start your journey by choosing one of three Pokémon . . .

QUAXLY

SPRIGATITO

FUECOCO

Once you have your first Pokémon, you can catch other Pokémon—and battle other Pokémon!

So get ready, Trainers. Soon you'll be prepared to master almost any Pokémon challenge! To keep learning, just turn the page . . .

WHAT ARE POKÉMON?

Pokémon are creatures that come in all shapes, sizes, and personalities.

They live in many types of areas, from oceans and rivers to mountains and caves, to forests and fields, and more. Trainers can find, capture, train, trade, collect, and use Pokémon in battle against rivals in the quest to become top Pokémon Trainers.

This book contains 400 known species of Pokémon who live in Paldea. For most species, there are many individual Pokémon. Some are very common, like Tauros, who live in herds. Others, like Koraidon and Miraidon, are classified as Legendary Pokémon, and are extremely rare.

Each individual Pokémon has its own personality. For example, there are a lot of Pikachu, but Ash has a very special one who travels with him on all his adventures.

A Trainer's goal is to befriend and catch Pokémon in the wild and then train them to battle one another. Pokémon do not get seriously hurt in battle. If they are defeated, they faint and then return to the Poké Balls to rest and be healed. A Trainer's job is to take good care of their Pokémon.

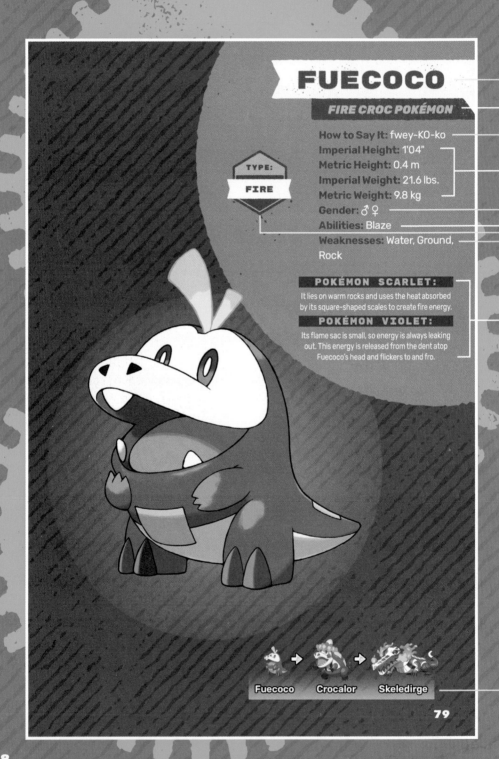

FUECOCO

FIRE CROC POKÉMON

How to Say It: fwey-KO-ko
Imperial Height: 1'04"
Metric Height: 0.4 m
Imperial Weight: 21.6 lbs.
Metric Weight: 9.8 kg
Gender: ♂ ♀
Abilities: Blaze
Weaknesses: Water, Ground, Rock

TYPE: FIRE

POKÉMON SCARLET:

It lies on warm rocks and uses the heat absorbed by its square-shaped scales to create fire energy.

POKÉMON VIOLET:

Its flame sac is small, so energy is always leaking out. This energy is released from the dent atop Fuecoco's head and flickers to and fro.

Fuecoco → Crocalor → Skeledirge

79

HOW TO USE THIS BOOK

This book will provide the basic stats and facts you need to know to start your Pokémon journey. Here's what you'll discover about each Pokémon:

SPECIES NAME

CATEGORY

All Pokémon belong to a certain species category.

TYPE

Each Pokémon has a type, and some even have two! (Pokémon with two types are called dual-type Pokémon.) Every Pokémon type comes with advantages and disadvantages.

HOW TO SAY IT

When it comes to Pokémon pronunciation, it's easy to get tongue-tied! There are many Pokémon with unusual names, so we'll help you sound them out. Soon you'll be saying Pokémon names so perfectly, you'll sound like a professor!

HEIGHT AND WEIGHT

How does each Pokémon measure up? Find out by checking its height and weight stats. And remember, good things come in all shapes and sizes. It's up to every Trainer to work with their Pokémon and play up its strengths.

GENDER

Most Pokémon are both male (♂) and female (♀), but some are exclusively one gender or have an unknown gender.

ABILITIES

Each Pokémon has an Ability that can help it in battle. A Pokémon's Ability usually relates back to its type in one way or another. Some Pokémon have one of two possible Abilities.

WEAKNESSES

In a battle, the effectiveness of a Pokémon's moves depends on the type of its opponent. A Pokémon's weaknesses show what other Pokémon types will most successfully be able to damage it in an attack!

DESCRIPTION

Knowledge is power! Pokémon Trainers have to know their stuff. Find out the specifics about your Pokémon species here.

EVOLUTION

If your Pokémon has an evolved form or pre-evolved form, we'll show you its place in the chain and how it evolves.

GUIDE TO POKÉMON TYPES

Type is the key to unlocking a Pokémon's power.

A Pokémon's type can tell you a lot about it—from where to find it in the wild to the moves it will be able to use on the battlefield. For example, Water-type Pokémon usually live in lakes, rivers, and oceans, and use moves like Bubble and Hydro Pump.

A clever Trainer should always consider type when picking a Pokémon for a match, because type shows a Pokémon's strengths and weaknesses. For example, a Fire type may melt an Ice type, but against a Water type, it might find it's the one in hot water. And while a Water type usually has the upper hand in battle with a Fire type, a Water-type move would only act like a sprinkler on a Grass-type Pokémon. But when that same Grass type is battling a Fire type, it just might get scorched.

BUG

DARK

FAIRY

ELECTRIC

FIGHTING

DRAGON

FLYING

FIRE

GHOST

GRASS

GROUND

ICE

NORMAL

PSYCHIC

ROCK

POISON

STEEL

WATER

11

BATTLE BASICS

WHY BATTLE?

There are two basic reasons for a Pokémon to battle. One is for sport. You can battle another Trainer in a friendly competition. Your Pokémon do the fighting, but you decide which Pokémon and which moves to use.

The second reason is to catch wild Pokémon. Wild Pokémon have no training and no owners. They can be found pretty much anywhere. Battle is one of the main ways to catch a Pokémon. But other Trainers' Pokémon are off-limits. You can't capture their Pokémon, even if you win a competition.

WHICH POKÉMON TO USE?

As you prepare for your first battle, you may have several Pokémon to choose from. Use the resources in this book to help you decide which Pokémon would be best. If you're facing a Fire type like Fuecoco, you can put out its sparks with a Water type like Quaxly.

THE FACE-OFF

You and your Pokémon will have to face and hopefully defeat each and every Pokémon on the other Trainer's team. You win when your Pokémon have defeated all the other Trainer's Pokémon. A Pokémon is defeated when it gets so weak it faints.

PALDEA REGION SPECIFICS

Each new region in the Pokémon world has its own unique climate and terrain where many newly discovered Pokémon live—along with plenty of previously discovered Pokémon who make their home there. In some regions, Pokémon can have special kinds of region-specific forms or Evolutions. Read on to learn about what is unique in the Paldea region!

THE TERASTRAL PHENOMENON

The Terastal phenomenon is an exciting new twist to Pokémon battles in Paldea. When Pokémon Terastallize in a battle, they become covered in a crystalline exterior and get a shining Tera Jewel above their head. Their type also changes to a Tera Type for the remainder of the battle, which makes their moves of that type stronger during battle. Terastallized Pokémon are exceptionally powerful.

TITAN POKÉMON AND HERBA MYSTICA

In Paldea, you might hunt down rare plants called Herba Mystica. These legendary herbs are scattered throughout the region—and they're guarded by Pokémon of unusual size and strength known as Titans. The Titan Pokémon must be defeated in battle if you want to claim the herbs. When Legendary Pokémon Koraidon and Miraidon eat the Herba Mystica, they gain new powers.

AND MUCH MORE!

Trainers can explore Paldea to unlock its secrets. From the mysterious Paradox Pokémon of the region to the four Legendary Pokémon known as the Treasures of Ruin, each sealed away in a shrine, there is so much to discover!

POKÉMON STATS AND FACTS

Ready for the essential info about every Pokémon found in the Paldea region?

TURN THE PAGE AND BEGIN!

ABOMASNOW

FROST TREE POKÉMON

How to Say It: ah-BOM-ah-snow
Imperial Height: 7'03"
Metric Height: 2.2 m
Imperial Weight: 298.7 lbs.
Metric Weight: 135.5 kg
Gender: ♂♀
Abilities: Snow Warning
Weaknesses: Steel, Fire, Flying, Poison, Fighting, Rock, Bug

TYPE:
GRASS-
ICE

POKÉMON SCARLET:

It lives a quiet life on mountains that are perpetually covered in snow. It hides itself by whipping up blizzards.

POKÉMON VIOLET:

They appear when the snow flowers bloom. When the petals fall, they retreat to places unknown again.

Snover → Abomasnow

ALOMOMOLA

CARING POKÉMON

TYPE:
WATER

How to Say It: uh-LOH-muh-MOH-luh
Imperial Height: 3'11"
Metric Height: 1.2 m
Imperial Weight: 69.7 lbs.
Metric Weight: 31.6 kg
Gender: ♂♀
Abilities: Hydration, Healer
Weaknesses: Grass, Electric

POKÉMON SCARLET:

It gently holds injured and weak Pokémon in its fins. Its special membrane heals their wounds.

POKÉMON VIOLET:

They float upon the open sea. Many water Pokémon gather in the area around Alomomola.

Does not evolve.

ALTARIA

HUMMING POKÉMON

TYPE:
DRAGON-FLYING

How to Say It: ahl-TAR-ee-uh
Imperial Height: 3'07"
Metric Height: 1.1 m
Imperial Weight: 45.4 lbs.
Metric Weight: 20.6 kg
Gender: ♂♀
Abilities: Natural Cure
Weaknesses: Fairy, Dragon, Ice, Rock

POKÉMON SCARLET:
If it bonds with a person, it will gently envelop the friend with its soft wings, then hum.

POKÉMON VIOLET:
On sunny days, it flies freely through the sky and blends into the clouds. It sings in a beautiful soprano.

Swablu → Altaria

AMOONGUSS

MUSHROOM POKÉMON

How to Say It: uh-MOON-gus
Imperial Height: 2'00"
Metric Height: 0.6 m
Imperial Weight: 23.1 lbs.
Metric Weight: 10.5 kg
Gender: ♂♀
Abilities: Effect Spore
Weaknesses: Fire, Psychic, Flying, Ice

TYPE:
GRASS-POISON

POKÉMON SCARLET:
Be wary of the poisonous spores it releases. Mushrooms resembling Amoonguss's caps will grow out of anywhere the spores touch.

POKÉMON VIOLET:
Amoonguss mimics Poké Balls. It is not yet clear whether this mimicry is effective against other Pokémon.

Foongus → Amoonguss

AMPHAROS

LIGHT POKÉMON

How to Say It: AMF-fah-rahs
Imperial Height: 4'07"
Metric Height: 1.4 m
Imperial Weight: 135.6 lbs.
Metric Weight: 61.5 kg
Gender: ♂♀
Abilities: Static
Weaknesses: Ground

TYPE: ELECTRIC

POKÉMON SCARLET:
The bright light on its tail can be seen far away. It has been treasured since ancient times as a beacon.

POKÉMON VIOLET:
When it gets dark, the light from its bright, shiny tail can be seen from far away on the ocean's surface.

Mareep ➡ Flaaffy ➡ Ampharos

ANNIHILAPE

RAGE MONKEY POKÉMON

How to Say It: uh-NEYE-uh-layp
Imperial Height: 3'11"
Metric Height: 1.2 m
Imperial Weight: 123.5 lbs.
Metric Weight: 56.0 kg
Gender: ♂♀
Abilities: Inner Focus, Vital Spirit
Weaknesses: Ghost, Psychic, Flying, Fairy

TYPE: FIGHTING-GHOST

POKÉMON SCARLET:
When its anger rose beyond a critical point, this Pokémon gained power that is unfettered by the limits of its physical body.

POKÉMON VIOLET:
It imbues its fists with the power of the rage that it kept hidden in its heart. Opponents struck by these imbued fists will be shattered to their core.

Mankey ➡ Primeape ➡ Annihilape

TYPE:
GRASS-DRAGON

APPLETUN
APPLE NECTAR POKÉMON

How to Say It: AP-pell-tun
Imperial Height: 1'04"
Metric Height: 0.4 m
Imperial Weight: 28.7 lbs.
Metric Weight: 13.0 kg
Gender: ♂♀
Abilities: Gluttony, Ripen
Weaknesses: Flying, Ice, Dragon, Poison, Fairy, Bug

POKÉMON SCARLET:
It feeds mainly on sweet apples. It will also eat small bug Pokémon that are attracted by its sweet nectar.

POKÉMON VIOLET:
When some Lechonk come along to lick the sweet nectar on Appletun's back, Appletun will spew sticky nectar at them to drive them away.

Applin → Appletun → Flapple

APPLIN
APPLE CORE POKÉMON

How to Say It: AP-lin
Imperial Height: 0'08"
Metric Height: 0.2 m
Imperial Weight: 1.1 lbs.
Metric Weight: 0.5 kg
Gender: ♂♀
Abilities: Gluttony, Ripen
Weaknesses: Flying, Ice, Dragon, Poison, Fairy, Bug

TYPE:
GRASS-DRAGON

POKÉMON SCARLET:
It grows by eating the flesh of an apple. Applin uses its own body fluid to strengthen the apple's skin and prevent it from rotting.

POKÉMON VIOLET:
Applin lives inside an apple. When an Applin is separated from its apple, its body loses moisture and the Pokémon grows weak.

Applin → Appletun → Flapple

ARBOLIVA

OLIVE POKÉMON

TYPE: GRASS-NORMAL

How to Say It: ar-bowl-EE-vuh
Imperial Height: 4'07"
Metric Height: 1.4 m
Imperial Weight: 106.3 lbs.
Metric Weight: 48.2 kg
Gender: ♂♀
Abilities: Seed Sower
Weaknesses: Ice, Fire, Flying, Poison, Fighting, Bug

POKÉMON SCARLET:

This calm Pokémon is very compassionate. It will share its delicious, nutrient-rich oil with weakened Pokémon.

POKÉMON VIOLET:

This Pokémon drives back enemies by launching its rich, aromatic oil at them with enough force to smash a boulder.

Smoliv → Dolliv → Arboliva

TYPE: FIRE

ARCANINE

LEGENDARY POKÉMON

How to Say It: ARE-ka-nine
Imperial Height: 6'03"
Metric Height: 1.9 m
Imperial Weight: 341.7 lbs.
Metric Weight: 155.0 kg
Gender: ♂♀
Abilities: Intimidate, Flash Fire
Weaknesses: Ground, Rock, Water

POKÉMON SCARLET:

An ancient picture scroll shows that people were captivated by its movement as it ran through prairies.

POKÉMON VIOLET:

Its magnificent bark conveys a sense of majesty. Anyone hearing it can't help but grovel before it.

Growlithe → Arcanine

ARCTIBAX

ICE FIN POKÉMON

TYPE: DRAGON-ICE

How to Say It: ARK-tuh-baks
Imperial Height: 2'07"
Metric Height: 0.8 m
Imperial Weight: 66.1 lbs.
Metric Weight: 30.0 kg
Gender: ♂♀
Abilities: Thermal Exchange
Weaknesses: Steel, Fairy, Rock Fighting, Dragon

POKÉMON SCARLET:

Arctibax freezes the air around it, protecting its face with an ice mask and turning its dorsal fin into a blade of ice.

POKÉMON VIOLET:

It attacks with the blade of its frozen dorsal fin by doing a front flip in the air. Arctibax's strong back and legs allow it to pull off this technique.

Frigibax → Arctibax → Baxcalibur

ARMAROUGE

FIRE WARRIOR POKÉMON

How to Say It: ARM-uh-roozh
Imperial Height: 4'11"
Metric Height: 1.5 m
Imperial Weight: 187.4 lbs.
Metric Weight: 85.0 kg
Gender: ♂♀
Abilities: Flash Fire
Weaknesses: Ground, Rock, Ghost, Water, Dark

TYPE: FIRE-PSYCHIC

POKÉMON SCARLET:

Armarouge evolved through the use of a set of armor that belonged to a distinguished warrior. This Pokémon is incredibly loyal.

POKÉMON VIOLET:

This Pokémon clads itself in armor that has been fortified by psychic and fire energy, and it shoots blazing fireballs.

Charcadet → Armarouge

ARROKUDA

RUSH POKÉMON

How to Say It: AIR-oh-KOO-duh
Imperial Height: 1'08"
Metric Height: 0.5 m
Imperial Weight: 2.2 lbs.
Metric Weight: 1.0 kg
Gender: ♂♀
Abilities: Swift Swim
Weaknesses: Grass, Electric

TYPE: WATER

POKÉMON SCARLET:

Arrokuda can swim quickly only in a straight line. The ones that become sluggish from overeating are the first to be targeted by flocks of Wattrel.

POKÉMON VIOLET:

It takes down prey by charging into them with its hard, pointed jaw. But Arrokuda's eyesight is poor, so this tactic has a low success rate.

Arrokuda   Barraskewda

AVALUGG

ICEBERG POKÉMON

How to Say It: AV-uh-lug
Imperial Height: 6'07"
Metric Height: 2.0 m
Imperial Weight: 1,113.3 lbs.
Metric Weight: 505.0 kg
Gender: ♂♀
Abilities: Own Tempo, Ice Body
Weaknesses: Fire, Steel, Fighting, Rock

TYPE: ICE

POKÉMON SCARLET:

As Avalugg walks along with Bergmite on its back, it comes across pods of Cetitan. It lets them pass to avoid conflict.

POKÉMON VIOLET:

This Pokémon uses its massive icy body to flatten anything that gets in its way. When it's floating out on the ocean, it looks exactly like drift ice.

Bergmite   Avalugg

AXEW

TUSK POKÉMON

TYPE:

DRAGON

How to Say It: AKS-yoo
Imperial Height: 2'00"
Metric Height: 0.6 m
Imperial Weight: 39.7 lbs.
Metric Weight: 18.0 kg
Gender: ♂♀
Abilities: Rivalry, Mold Breaker
Weaknesses: Ice, Dragon, Fairy

POKÉMON SCARLET:

This Pokémon lives in nests that are made in the ground. People in ancient times used its tusks as cooking knives.

POKÉMON VIOLET:

If you see peculiar teeth marks on boulders or trees, it means an Axew is likely living nearby.

Axew → Fraxure → Haxorus

AZUMARILL

AQUA RABBIT POKÉMON

How to Say It: ah-ZU-mare-rill
Imperial Height: 2'07"
Metric Height: 0.8 m
Imperial Weight: 62.8 lbs.
Metric Weight: 28.5 kg
Gender: ♂♀
Abilities: Thick Fat, Huge Power
Weaknesses: Grass, Electric, Poison

TYPE:

WATER-FAIRY

POKÉMON SCARLET:

Its long ears are superb sensors. It can distinguish the movements of things in water and tell what they are.

POKÉMON VIOLET:

By keeping still and listening intently, it can tell what is in even wild, fast-moving rivers.

Azurill → Marill → Azumarill

AZURILL

POLKA DOT POKÉMON

How to Say It: uh-ZOO-rill
Imperial Height: 0'08"
Metric Height: 0.2 m
Imperial Weight: 4.4 lbs.
Metric Weight: 2.0 kg
Gender: ♂♀
Abilities: Thick Fat, Huge Power
Weaknesses: Steel, Poison

TYPE:
NORMAL-
FAIRY

POKÉMON SCARLET:

Its tail bounces like a rubber ball. It flings that tail around to fight opponents bigger than itself.

POKÉMON VIOLET:

Its tail is packed full of the nutrients it needs to grow.

Azurill → **Marill** → **Azumarill**

BAGON

ROCK HEAD POKÉMON

TYPE:
DRAGON

How to Say It: BAY-gon
Imperial Height: 2'00"
Metric Height: 0.6 m
Imperial Weight: 92.8 lbs.
Metric Weight: 42.1 kg
Gender: ♂♀
Abilities: Rock Head
Weaknesses: Fairy, Ice, Dragon

POKÉMON SCARLET:

Its steel-hard head can shatter boulders. It longingly hopes for wings to grow so it can fly.

POKÉMON VIOLET:

Its belief that it will be able to fly one day is apparently the influence of information carried in its genes.

Bagon → **Shelgon** → **Salamence**

BANETTE

MARIONETTE POKÉMON

TYPE:
GHOST

How to Say It: bane-NETT
Imperial Height: 3'07"
Metric Height: 1.1 m
Imperial Weight: 27.6 lbs.
Metric Weight: 12.5 kg
Gender: ♂♀
Abilities: Insomnia, Frisk
Weaknesses: Ghost, Dark

POKÉMON SCARLET:
This Pokémon developed from an abandoned doll that amassed a grudge. It is seen in dark alleys.

POKÉMON VIOLET:
Strong feelings of hatred turned a puppet into a Pokémon. If it opens its mouth, its cursed energy escapes.

Shuppet ➡ Banette

BARBOACH

WHISKERS POKÉMON

TYPE:
WATER-GROUND

How to Say It: bar-BOACH
Imperial Height: 1'04"
Metric Height: 0.4 m
Imperial Weight: 4.2 lbs.
Metric Weight: 1.9 kg
Gender: ♂♀
Abilities: Oblivious, Anticipation
Weaknesses: Grass

POKÉMON SCARLET:
Its two whiskers provide a sensitive radar. Even in muddy waters, it can detect its prey's location.

POKÉMON VIOLET:
It probes muddy riverbeds with its two long whiskers. A slimy film protects its body.

Barboach ➡ Whiscash

BARRASKEWDA

SKEWER POKÉMON

How to Say It: BAIR-uh-SKYOO-duh
Imperial Height: 4'03"
Metric Height: 1.3 m
Imperial Weight: 66.1 lbs.
Metric Weight: 30.0 kg
Gender: ♂♀
Abilities: Swift Swim
Weaknesses: Grass, Electric

TYPE: WATER

POKÉMON SCARLET:

It spins its tail fins to leap from the water, then viciously bites down on Wingull flying close to the water's surface.

POKÉMON VIOLET:

It swims at speeds of over 100 knots and battles fiercely with pods of Finizen over prey.

Arrokuda → Barraskewda

BASCULIN

HOSTILE POKÉMON

RED-STRIPED FORM

BLUE-STRIPED FORM

Does not evolve.

TYPE: WATER

How to Say It: BASS-kyoo-lin
Imperial Height: 3'03"
Metric Height: 1.0 m
Imperial Weight: 39.7 lbs.
Metric Weight: 18.0 kg
Gender: ♂♀
Abilities: Reckless, Adaptability
Weaknesses: Grass, Electric

POKÉMON SCARLET:

Its temperament is vicious and aggressive. This Pokémon is also full of vitality and can multiply rapidly before anyone notices.

POKÉMON VIOLET:

It's so vicious that it's called the Thug of the River. Yet Basculin is still targeted by predators, such as Dondozo and Bombirdier.

BAXCALIBUR

ICE DRAGON POKÉMON

TYPE:
DRAGON-ICE

How to Say It: bak-SKA-leh-burr
Imperial Height: 6'11"
Metric Height: 2.1 m
Imperial Weight: 463.0 lbs.
Metric Weight: 210.0 kg
Gender: ♂♀
Abilities: Thermal Exchange
Weaknesses: Steel, Fairy, Rock, Fighting, Dragon

Frigibax → **Arctibax** → **Baxcalibur**

POKÉMON SCARLET:
This Pokémon blasts cryogenic air out from its mouth. This air can instantly freeze even liquid-hot lava.

POKÉMON VIOLET:
It launches itself into battle by flipping upside down and spewing frigid air from its mouth. It finishes opponents off with its dorsal blade.

BEARTIC

FREEZING POKÉMON

TYPE:
ICE

How to Say It: BAIR-tick
Imperial Height: 8'06"
Metric Height: 2.6 m
Imperial Weight: 573.2 lbs.
Metric Weight: 260.0 kg
Gender: ♂♀
Abilities: Snow Cloak, Slush Rush
Weaknesses: Fire, Fighting, Rock, Steel

POKÉMON SCARLET:
It is a ferocious, carnivorous Pokémon. Once it captures its prey, it will breathe cold air onto the prey to freeze and preserve it.

POKÉMON VIOLET:
Feared as the Snow-White Demon in northern lands, Beartic uses its frosty claws and fangs to attack prey.

Cubchoo → **Beartic**

BELLIBOLT

ELEFROG POKÉMON

How to Say It: BELL-ee-bolt
Imperial Height: 3'11"
Metric Height: 1.2 m
Imperial Weight: 249.1 lbs.
Metric Weight: 113.0 kg
Gender: ♂♀
Abilities: Static, Electromorphosis
Weaknesses: Ground

TYPE: ELECTRIC

POKÉMON SCARLET:

When this Pokémon expands and contracts its wobbly body, the belly-button dynamo in its stomach produces a huge amount of electricity.

POKÉMON VIOLET:

What appear to be eyeballs are actually organs for discharging the electricity generated by Bellibolt's belly-button dynamo.

Tadbulb → Bellibolt

BERGMITE

ICE CHUNK POKÉMON

TYPE: ICE

How to Say It: BERG-mite
Imperial Height: 3'03"
Metric Height: 1.0 m
Imperial Weight: 219.4 lbs.
Metric Weight: 99.5 kg
Gender: ♂♀
Abilities: Own Tempo, Ice Body
Weaknesses: Fire, Steel, Fighting, Rock

POKÉMON SCARLET:

They live in mountainous regions of frigid cold. On rare occasions, they ride on the back of an Avalugg to cross seas and move to new habitats.

POKÉMON VIOLET:

Bergmite protects itself by coating its body in ice formed by frigid air of −148 degrees Fahrenheit. It fights with Frigibax whenever they meet.

Bergmite → Avalugg

BISHARP

SWORD BLADE POKÉMON

TYPE: DARK-STEEL

How to Say It: BIH-sharp
Imperial Height: 5'03"
Metric Height: 1.6 m
Imperial Weight: 154.3 lbs.
Metric Weight: 70.0 kg
Gender: ♂♀
Abilities: Inner Focus, Defiant
Weaknesses: Fighting, Fire, Ground

POKÉMON SCARLET:

This Pokémon commands a group of several Pawniard. Groups that are defeated in territorial disputes are absorbed by the winning side.

POKÉMON VIOLET:

Bisharp mercilessly cuts its opponents to pieces with the sharp blades covering its body. It will do anything to win.

Pawniard → **Bisharp** → **Kingambit**

BLISSEY

HAPPINESS POKÉMON

How to Say It: BLISS-sey
Imperial Height: 4'11"
Metric Height: 1.5 m
Imperial Weight: 103.2 lbs.
Metric Weight: 46.8 kg
Gender: ♀
Abilities: Natural Cure, Serene Grace
Weaknesses: Fighting

TYPE: NORMAL

POKÉMON SCARLET:

Anyone who takes even one taste of Blissey's egg becomes unfailingly caring and pleasant to everyone.

POKÉMON VIOLET:

The eggs it lays are filled with happiness. Eating even one bite will bring a smile to anyone.

Happiny → **Chansey** → **Blissey**

BOMBIRDIER

How to Say It: BAHM-burr-deer
Imperial Height: 4'11"
Metric Height: 1.5 m
Imperial Weight: 94.6 lbs.
Metric Weight: 42.9 kg
Gender: ♂♀
Abilities: Keen Eye, Big Pecks
Weaknesses: Fairy, Electric, Ice, Rock

TYPE: FLYING-DARK

POKÉMON SCARLET:
It gathers things up in an apron made from shed feathers added to the Pokémon's chest feathers, then drops those things from high places for fun.

POKÉMON VIOLET:
Bombirdier uses the apron on its chest to bundle up food, which it carries back to its nest. It enjoys dropping things that make loud noises.

Does not evolve.

BONSLY

TYPE: ROCK

How to Say It: BON-slye
Imperial Height: 1'08"
Metric Height: 0.5 m
Imperial Weight: 33.1 lbs.
Metric Weight: 15.0 kg
Gender: ♂♀
Abilities: Rock Head, Sturdy
Weaknesses: Fighting, Grass, Ground, Steel, Water

POKÉMON SCARLET:
In order to adjust the level of fluids in its body, it exudes water from its eyes. This makes it appear to be crying.

POKÉMON VIOLET:
From its eyes, it can expel excess moisture from its body. This liquid is similar in composition to human sweat.

Bonsly Sudowoodo

BOUNSWEET

FRUIT POKÉMON

TYPE:
GRASS

How to Say It: BOWN*-sweet
(*Rhymes with DOWN)
Imperial Height: 1'00"
Metric Height: 0.3 m
Imperial Weight: 7.1 lbs.
Metric Weight: 3.2 kg
Gender: ♀
Abilities: Oblivious, Leaf Guard
Weaknesses: Fire, Flying, Ice,
Poison, Bug

POKÉMON SCARLET:

Its sweat is sweet, like syrup made from boiled-down fruit. Because of this, Bounsweet was highly valued in the past, when sweeteners were scarce.

POKÉMON VIOLET:

A Greedent drawn in by the sweet scent of these Pokémon will tuck the Bounsweet in among the berries in its tail and carry them all away.

Bounsweet → Steenee → Tsareena

BRAMBLEGHAST

TUMBLEWEED POKÉMON

How to Say It: BRAM-bull-gast
Imperial Height: 3'11"
Metric Height: 1.2 m
Imperial Weight: 13.2 lbs.
Metric Weight: 6.0 kg
Gender: ♂♀
Abilities: Wind Rider
Weaknesses: Ghost, Fire,
Flying, Dark, Ice

TYPE:
GRASS-GHOST

POKÉMON SCARLET:

It will open the branches of its head to envelop its prey. Once it absorbs all the life energy it needs, it expels the prey and discards it.

POKÉMON VIOLET:

Brambleghast wanders around arid regions. On rare occasions, mass outbreaks of these Pokémon will bury an entire town.

Bramblin → Brambleghast

BRAMBLIN

TUMBLEWEED POKÉMON

How to Say It: BRAM-bah-lihn
Imperial Height: 2'00"
Metric Height: 0.6 m
Imperial Weight: 1.3 lbs.
Metric Weight: 0.6 kg
Gender: ♂♀
Abilities: Wind Rider
Weaknesses: Ghost, Fire, Flying, Dark, Ice

TYPE: GRASS-GHOST

POKÉMON SCARLET:

A soul unable to move on to the afterlife was blown around by the wind until it got tangled up with dried grass and became a Pokémon.

POKÉMON VIOLET:

Not even Bramblin knows where it is headed as it tumbles across the wilderness, blown by the wind. It loathes getting wet.

Bramblin → **Brambleghast**

BRAVIARY

VALIANT POKÉMON

How to Say It: BRAY-vee-air-ee
Imperial Height: 4'11"
Metric Height: 1.5 m
Imperial Weight: 90.4 lbs.
Metric Weight: 41.0 kg
Gender: ♂
Abilities: Keen Eye, Sheer Force
Weaknesses: Electric, Ice, Rock

TYPE: NORMAL-FLYING

POKÉMON SCARLET:

The more scars they have, the more respect these brave soldiers of the sky get from their peers.

POKÉMON VIOLET:

For the sake of its friends, this brave warrior of the sky will not stop battling, even if injured.

Rufflet → **Braviary**

BRELOOM

MUSHROOM POKÉMON

How to Say It: brell-LOOM
Imperial Height: 3'11"
Metric Height: 1.2 m
Imperial Weight: 86.4 lbs.
Metric Weight: 39.2 kg
Gender: ♂ ♀
Abilities: Effect Spore, Poison Heal
Weaknesses: Fire, Psychic, Flying, Ice, Poison, Fairy

TYPE:
GRASS-FIGHTING

POKÉMON SCARLET:
It scatters poisonous spores and throws powerful punches while its foe is hampered by inhaled spores.

POKÉMON VIOLET:
The seeds on its tail are made of toxic spores. It knocks out foes with quick, virtually invisible punches.

Shroomish → **Breloom**

BRONZONG

BRONZE BELL POKÉMON

TYPE:
STEEL-PSYCHIC

How to Say It: brawn-ZONG
Imperial Height: 4'03"
Metric Height: 1.3 m
Imperial Weight: 412.3 lbs.
Metric Weight: 187.0 kg
Gender: Unknown
Abilities: Levitate, Heatproof
Weaknesses: Fire, Ground, Ghost, Dark

POKÉMON SCARLET:
In ages past, this Pokémon was revered as a bringer of rain. It was found buried in the ground.

POKÉMON VIOLET:
It brought rains by opening portals to another world. It was revered as a bringer of plentiful harvests.

Bronzor → **Bronzong**

BRONZOR

BRONZE POKÉMON

How to Say It: BRAWN-zor
Imperial Height: 1'08"
Metric Height: 0.5 m
Imperial Weight: 133.4 lbs.
Metric Weight: 60.5 kg
Gender: Unknown
Abilities: Levitate, Heatproof
Weaknesses: Fire, Ground, Ghost, Dark

TYPE:
STEEL-PSYCHIC

POKÉMON SCARLET:

Ancient people believed that the pattern on Bronzor's back contained a mysterious power.

POKÉMON VIOLET:

They are found in ancient tombs. The patterns on their backs are said to be imbued with mysterious power.

Bronzor → Bronzong

BRUTE BONNET

PARADOX POKÉMON

TYPE:
GRASS-DARK

How to Say It: BRUTE BAW-net
Imperial Height: 3'11"
Metric Height: 1.2 m
Imperial Weight: 46.3 lbs.
Metric Weight: 21.0 kg
Gender: Unknown
Abilities: Protosynthesis
Weaknesses: Ice, Fire, Flying, Poison, Fighting, Fairy, Bug

POKÉMON SCARLET:

It is possible that the creature listed as Brute Bonnet in a certain book could actually be this Pokémon.

POKÉMON VIOLET:

It bears a slight resemblance to a Pokémon described in a dubious magazine as a cross between a dinosaur and a mushroom.

Does not evolve.

BRUXISH

GNASH TEETH POKÉMON

TYPE:
WATER-PSYCHIC

How to Say It: BRUCK-sish
Imperial Height: 2'11"
Metric Height: 0.9 m
Imperial Weight: 41.9 lbs.
Metric Weight: 19.0 kg
Gender: ♂♀
Abilities: Strong Jaw, Dazzling
Weaknesses: Ghost, Dark, Grass, Electric, Bug

POKÉMON SCARLET:
It grinds its teeth with great force to stimulate its brain. It fires the psychic energy created by this process from the protuberance on its head.

POKÉMON VIOLET:
When sunlight reflects on the ripples created by a Bruxish grinding its teeth, the water all around sparkles brilliantly.

Does not evolve.

BUIZEL

SEA WEASEL POKÉMON

TYPE:
WATER

How to Say It: BWEE-zul
Imperial Height: 2'04"
Metric Height: 0.7 m
Imperial Weight: 65.0 lbs.
Metric Weight: 29.5 kg
Gender: ♂♀
Abilities: Swift Swim
Weaknesses: Grass, Electric

POKÉMON SCARLET:
It spins its two tails like a screw to propel itself through water. The tails also slice clinging seaweed.

POKÉMON VIOLET:
It inflates its flotation sac, keeping its face above water in order to watch for prey movement.

Buizel ⇨ **Floatzel**

CACNEA

CACTUS POKÉMON

How to Say It: CACK-nee-uh
Imperial Height: 1'04"
Metric Height: 0.4 m
Imperial Weight: 113.1 lbs.
Metric Weight: 51.3 kg
Gender: ♂♀
Abilities: Sand Veil
Weaknesses: Fire, Flying, Ice, Poison, Bug

TYPE: GRASS

POKÉMON SCARLET:

It prefers harsh environments, such as deserts. It can survive for 30 days on water stored in its body.

POKÉMON VIOLET:

It lives in arid locations. Its yellow flowers bloom once a year.

Cacnea → Cacturne

CACTURNE

SCARECROW POKÉMON

How to Say It: CACK-turn
Imperial Height: 4'03"
Metric Height: 1.3 m
Imperial Weight: 170.6 lbs.
Metric Weight: 77.4 kg
Gender: ♂♀
Abilities: Sand Veil
Weaknesses: Ice, Fire, Flying, Poison, Fighting, Fairy, Bug

TYPE: GRASS-DARK

Cacnea → Cacturne

POKÉMON SCARLET:

Packs of them follow travelers through the desert until the travelers can no longer move.

POKÉMON VIOLET:

It lives in deserts. It becomes active at night when it hunts for prey exhausted from the desert's heat.

CAMERUPT

ERUPTION POKÉMON

TYPE:
FIRE-GROUND

How to Say It: CAM-err-rupt
Imperial Height: 6'03"
Metric Height: 1.9 m
Imperial Weight: 485.0 lbs.
Metric Weight: 220.0 kg
Gender: ♂♀
Abilities: Magma Armor, Solid Rock
Weaknesses: Water, Ground

POKÉMON SCARLET:

It lives in the crater of a volcano. It is well known that the humps on its back erupt every 10 years.

POKÉMON VIOLET:

If angered, the humps on its back erupt in a shower of molten lava. It lives in the craters of volcanoes.

Numel → **Camerupt**

CAPSAKID

SPICY PEPPER POKÉMON

How to Say It: KAP-suh-KID
Imperial Height: 1'00"
Metric Height: 0.3 m
Imperial Weight: 6.6 lbs.
Metric Weight: 3.0 kg
Gender: ♂♀
Abilities: Chlorophyll, Insomnia
Weaknesses: Fire, Flying, Ice, Poison, Bug

TYPE:
GRASS

POKÉMON SCARLET:

The more sunlight this Pokémon bathes in, the more spicy chemicals are produced by its body, and thus the spicier its moves become.

POKÉMON VIOLET:

Traditional Paldean dishes can be extremely spicy because they include the shed front teeth of Capsakid among their ingredients.

Capsakid → **Scovillain**

CARKOL

COAL POKÉMON

How to Say It: KAR-kohl
Imperial Height: 3'07"
Metric Height: 1.1 m
Imperial Weight: 172.0 lbs.
Metric Weight: 78.0 kg
Gender: ♂♀
Abilities: Flame Body, Steam Engine
Weaknesses: Water, Ground, Fighting, Rock

**TYPE:
ROCK-
FIRE**

POKÉMON SCARLET:

The temperature inside its body increases when it experiences strong emotions. It rolls around frantically while spewing flames.

POKÉMON VIOLET:

Due to the coal tar created inside it, the heap of coal on Carkol's back never falls apart, even when the Pokémon rolls around at high speeds.

Rolycoly → Carkol → Coalossal

CERULEDGE

FIRE BLADES POKÉMON

**TYPE:
FIRE-
GHOST**

How to Say It: suh-ROOL-ehj
Imperial Height: 5'03"
Metric Height: 1.6 m
Imperial Weight: 136.7 lbs.
Metric Weight: 62.0 kg
Gender: ♂♀
Abilities: Flash Fire
Weaknesses: Water, Ghost, Ground, Dark, Rock

POKÉMON SCARLET:

The fiery blades on its arms burn fiercely with the lingering resentment of a sword wielder who fell before accomplishing their goal.

POKÉMON VIOLET:

An old set of armor steeped in grudges caused this Pokémon's evolution. Ceruledge cuts its enemies to pieces without mercy.

Charcadet → Ceruledge

CETITAN

TERRA WHALE POKÉMON

TYPE: ICE

How to Say It: sih-TYE-tun
Imperial Height: 14'09"
Metric Height: 4.5 m
Imperial Weight: 1,543.2 lbs.
Metric Weight: 700.0 kg
Gender: ♂♀
Abilities: Thick Fat, Sludge Rush
Weaknesses: Fire, Steel, Fighting, Rock

POKÉMON SCARLET:

This Pokémon wanders around snowy, icy areas. It protects its body with powerful muscles and a thick layer of fat under its skin.

POKÉMON VIOLET:

Ice energy builds up in the horn on its upper jaw, causing the horn to reach cryogenic temperatures that freeze its surroundings.

Cetoddle → Cetitan

CETODDLE

TERRA WHALE POKÉMON

How to Say It: sih-TAH-dul
Imperial Height: 3'11"
Metric Height: 1.2 m
Imperial Weight: 99.2 lbs.
Metric Weight: 45.0 kg
Gender: ♂♀
Abilities: Thick Fat, Snow Cloak
Weaknesses: Fire, Steel, Fighting, Rock

TYPE: ICE

POKÉMON SCARLET:

This species left the ocean and began living on land a very long time ago. It seems to be closely related to Wailmer.

POKÉMON VIOLET:

It lives in frigid regions in pods of five or so individuals. It loves the minerals found in snow and ice.

Cetoddle → Cetitan

CHANSEY

EGG POKÉMON

How to Say It: CHAN-see
Imperial Height: 3'07"
Metric Height: 1.1 m
Imperial Weight: 76.3 lbs.
Metric Weight: 34.6 kg
Gender: ♀
Abilities: Natural Cure, Serene Grace
Weaknesses: Fighting

**TYPE:
NORMAL**

POKÉMON SCARLET:

This kindly Pokémon lays highly nutritious eggs and shares them with injured Pokémon or people.

POKÉMON VIOLET:

It walks carefully to prevent its egg from breaking. However, it is extremely fast at running away.

Happiny → Chansey → Blissey

CHARCADET

FIRE CHILD POKÉMON

**TYPE:
FIRE**

How to Say It: CHAR-kuh-deht
Imperial Height: 2'00"
Metric Height: 0.6 m
Imperial Weight: 23.1 lbs.
Metric Weight: 10.5 kg
Gender: ♂ ♀
Abilities: Flash Fire
Weaknesses: Water, Ground, Rock

POKÉMON SCARLET:

Burnt charcoal came to life and became a Pokémon. Possessing a fiery fighting spirit, Charcadet will battle even tough opponents.

POKÉMON VIOLET:

Its firepower increases when it fights, reaching over 1,800 degrees Fahrenheit. It likes berries that are rich in fat.

Armarouge

Charcadet

Ceruledge

CHEWTLE

SNAPPING POKÉMON

TYPE:
WATER

How to Say It: CHOO-tull
Imperial Height: 1'00"
Metric Height: 0.3 m
Imperial Weight: 18.7 lbs.
Metric Weight: 8.5 kg
Gender: ♂ ♀
Abilities: Shell Armor, Strong Jaw
Weaknesses: Grass, Electric

POKÉMON SCARLET:

Its large front tooth is still growing in. When the tooth itches, this Pokémon will bite another Chewtle's horn, and the two Pokémon will tussle.

POKÉMON VIOLET:

A popular game among children is to lift up sticks that Chewtle have bitten on to see whose Chewtle can hang on the longest.

Chewtle → **Drednaw**

CHI-YU

LEGENDARY POKÉMON

RUINOUS POKÉMON

How to Say It: CHEE-yoo
Imperial Height: 1'04"
Metric Height: 0.4 m
Imperial Weight: 10.8 lbs.
Metric Weight: 4.9 kg
Gender: Unknown
Abilities: Beads of Ruin
Weaknesses: Water, Ground, Fighting, Rock

TYPE:
DARK-FIRE

POKÉMON SCARLET:

It controls flames burning at over 5,400 degrees Fahrenheit. It casually swims through the sea of lava it creates by melting rock and sand.

POKÉMON VIOLET:

The envy accumulated within curved beads that sparked multiple conflicts has clad itself in fire and become a Pokémon.

Does not evolve.

CHIEN-PAO

LEGENDARY POKÉMON

RUINOUS POKÉMON

How to Say It: CHYEHN-pow
Imperial Height: 6'03"
Metric Height: 1.9 m
Imperial Weight: 335.5 lbs.
Metric Weight: 152.2 kg
Gender: Unknown
Abilities: Sword of Ruin
Weaknesses: Steel, Fire, Fighting, Rock, Fairy, Bug

TYPE: DARK-ICE

POKÉMON SCARLET:
This Pokémon can control 100 tons of fallen snow. It plays around innocently by leaping in and out of avalanches it has caused.

POKÉMON VIOLET:
The hatred of those who perished by the sword long ago has clad itself in snow and become a Pokémon.

Does not evolve.

CLAUNCHER

WATER GUN POKÉMON

TYPE: WATER

How to Say It: CLAWN-chur
Imperial Height: 1'08"
Metric Height: 0.5 m
Imperial Weight: 18.3 lbs.
Metric Weight: 8.3 kg
Gender: ♂♀
Abilities: Mega Launcher
Weaknesses: Grass, Electric

POKÉMON SCARLET:
This Pokémon launches water by detonating gas inside its right claw. It snipes flying Pokémon.

POKÉMON VIOLET:
Claggcher's claws will regrow if they fall off. The meat inside the claws is edible, but it has a distinct flavor that doesn't appeal to all tastes.

Claggcher → **Clawitzer**

CLAWITZER

HOWITZER POKÉMON

TYPE:
WATER

How to Say It: CLOW-wit-zur
Imperial Height: 4'03"
Metric Height: 1.3 m
Imperial Weight: 77.8 lbs.
Metric Weight: 35.3 kg
Gender: ♂♀
Abilities: Mega Launcher
Weaknesses: Grass, Electric

POKÉMON SCARLET:

Clawitzer can move through the water at a speed of 60 knots by using gas inside its body to expel water from the back of its claw.

POKÉMON VIOLET:

The cannonballs of seawater that Clawitzer launches from its claw are powerful enough to punch through tanker hulls.

Clahuncher → **Clawitzer**

CLODSIRE

SPINY FISH POKÉMON

TYPE:
POISON-GROUND

How to Say It: KLAWD-seye-er
Imperial Height: 5'11"
Metric Height: 1.8 m
Imperial Weight: 491.6 lbs.
Metric Weight: 223.0 kg
Gender: ♂♀
Abilities: Poison Point, Water Absorb
Weaknesses: Water, Psychic, Ice, Ground

POKÉMON SCARLET:

When attacked, this Pokémon will retaliate by sticking thick spines out from its body. It's a risky move that puts everything on the line.

POKÉMON VIOLET:

It lives at the bottom of ponds and swamps. It will carry Wooper on its back and ferry them across water from one shore to the other.

Paldean Wooper → **Clodsire**

CLOYSTER

BIVALVE POKÉMON

How to Say It: CLOY-stur
Imperial Height: 4'11"
Metric Height: 1.5 m
Imperial Weight: 292.1 lbs.
Metric Weight: 132.5 kg
Gender: ♂♀
Abilities: Shell Armor, Skill Link
Weaknesses: Electric, Fighting, Grass, Rock

TYPE: WATER-ICE

POKÉMON SCARLET:
Cloyster that live in seas with harsh tidal currents grow large, sharp spikes on their shells.

POKÉMON VIOLET:
When attacked, it launches its spikes in quick volleys. Its innards have never been seen.

Shellder → Cloyster

COALOSSAL

COAL POKÉMON

TYPE: ROCK-FIRE

How to Say It: koh-LAHS-ull
Imperial Height: 9'02"
Metric Height: 2.8 m
Imperial Weight: 684.5 lbs.
Metric Weight: 310.5 kg
Gender: ♂♀
Abilities: Flame Body, Steam Engine
Weaknesses: Water, Ground, Fighting, Rock

Rolycoly → Carkol → Coalossal

POKÉMON SCARLET:
To intimidate its opponents, Coalossal will vigorously shake its body, scattering coal from its smoldering back.

POKÉMON VIOLET:
It's gentle usually but fearsome when angered. With a body that burns at over 2,700 degrees Fahrenheit, it crushes foes and turns them to ash.

COMBEE

TINY BEE POKÉMON

TYPE:
BUG-FLYING

How to Say It: COMB-bee
Imperial Height: 1'00"
Metric Height: 0.3 m
Imperial Weight: 12.1 lbs.
Metric Weight: 5.5 kg
Gender: ♂♀
Abilities: Honey Gather
Weaknesses: Rock, Electric, Fire, Flying, Ice

POKÉMON SCARLET:
At night, Combee sleep in a group of about a hundred, packed closely together in a lump.

POKÉMON VIOLET:
The trio is together from birth. It constantly gathers nectar from flowers to please Vespiquen.

Combee → Vespiquen

COPPERAJAH

TYPE:
STEEL

COPPERDERM POKÉMON

How to Say It: KAH-peh-RAH-zhah
Imperial Height: 9'10"
Metric Height: 3.0 m
Imperial Weight: 1,433.0 lbs.
Metric Weight: 650.0 kg
Gender: ♂♀
Abilities: Sheer Force
Weaknesses: Fire, Fighting, Ground

POKÉMON SCARLET:
This Pokémon was brought to Paldea long ago by people from a faraway land. It's so strong that it can easily pull an airplane.

POKÉMON VIOLET:
Copperajah are prideful, cantankerous Pokémon. Specimens with vibrant green skin command the respect of others of their kind.

Cufant Copperajah

CORVIKNIGHT

RAVEN POKÉMON

How to Say It: KOR-vih-nyte
Imperial Height: 7'03"
Metric Height: 2.2 m
Imperial Weight: 165.3 lbs.
Metric Weight: 75.0 kg
Gender: ♂♀
Abilities: Pressure, Unnerve
Weaknesses: Fire, Electric

TYPE:
FLYING-STEEL

POKÉMON SCARLET:

Corviknight can't serve as a taxi service in Paldea because the Pokémon's natural predators will attack it while it flies, endangering the customer.

POKÉMON VIOLET:

Although its wings have partly turned to steel and become heavy as a result, this Pokémon flies through the skies with ease.

Rookidee → **Corvisquire** → **Corviknight**

CORVISQUIRE

RAVEN POKÉMON

How to Say It: KOR-vih-skwyre
Imperial Height: 2'07"
Metric Height: 0.8 m
Imperial Weight: 35.3 lbs.
Metric Weight: 16.0 kg
Gender: ♂♀
Abilities: Keen Eye, Unnerve
Weaknesses: Electric, Ice, Rock

TYPE:
FLYING

POKÉMON SCARLET:

It's said that the reason behind Corvisquire's high level of intelligence is the large size of its brain relative to those of other bird Pokémon.

POKÉMON VIOLET:

This intelligent Pokémon will quickly learn how to use any tool it can hold in its beak or its talons.

Rookidee → **Corvisquire** → **Corviknight**

CRABOMINABLE

WOOLLY CRAB POKÉMON

How to Say It: crab-BAH-min-uh-bull
Imperial Height: 5'07"
Metric Height: 1.7 m
Imperial Weight: 396.8 lbs.
Metric Weight: 180.0 kg
Gender: ♂♀
Abilities: Hyper Cutter, Iron Fist
Weaknesses: Steel, Fire, Psychic, Flying, Fighting, Fairy

POKÉMON SCARLET:

The detached pincers of these Pokémon are delicious. Some Trainers bring Lechonk into the mountains just to search for them.

POKÉMON VIOLET:

Though its punches are powerful, this Pokémon's movements are sluggish. It blows icy bubbles from its mouth to immobilize its opponents.

Crabrawler → Crabominable

CRABRAWLER

BOXING POKÉMON

How to Say It: crab-BRAW-ler
Imperial Height: 2'00"
Metric Height: 0.6 m
Imperial Weight: 15.4 lbs.
Metric Weight: 7.0 kg
Gender: ♂♀
Abilities: Hyper Cutter, Iron Fist
Weaknesses: Psychic, Flying, Fairy

POKÉMON SCARLET:

This Pokémon punches trees and eats the berries that drop down, training itself and getting food at the same time.

POKÉMON VIOLET:

If it loses its pincers, they'll quickly regrow. The pincers are popular ingredients in paella since their shells produce a tasty soup stock.

Crabrawler → Crabominable

CROAGUNK

TOXIC MOUTH POKÉMON

How to Say It: CROW-gunk
Imperial Height: 2'04"
Metric Height: 0.7 m
Imperial Weight: 50.7 lbs.
Metric Weight: 23.0 kg
Gender: ♂♀
Abilities: Anticipation, Dry Skin
Weaknesses: Psychic, Flying, Ground

TYPE: POISON-FIGHTING

POKÉMON SCARLET:

Inflating its poison sacs, it fills the area with an odd sound and hits flinching opponents with a poison jab.

POKÉMON VIOLET:

It rarely fights fairly, but that is strictly to ensure survival. It is popular as a mascot.

Croagunk → Toxicroak

CROCALOR

FIRE CROC POKÉMON

TYPE: FIRE

How to Say It: KROCK-uh-lor
Imperial Height: 3'03"
Metric Height: 1.0 m
Imperial Weight: 67.7 lbs.
Metric Weight: 30.7 kg
Gender: ♂♀
Abilities: Blaze
Weaknesses: Water, Ground, Rock

POKÉMON SCARLET:

The combination of Crocalor's fire energy and overflowing vitality has caused an egg-shaped fireball to appear on the Pokémon's head.

POKÉMON VIOLET:

The valve in Crocalor's flame sac is closely connected to its vocal cords. This Pokémon utters a guttural cry as it spews flames every which way.

Fuecoco → Crocalor → Skeledirge

CRYOGONAL

TYPE: ICE

CRYSTALLIZING POKÉMON

How to Say It: kry-AH-guh-nul
Imperial Height: 3'07"
Metric Height: 1.1 m
Imperial Weight: 326.3 lbs.
Metric Weight: 148.0 kg
Gender: Unknown
Abilities: Levitate
Weaknesses: Fire, Steel, Fighting, Rock

POKÉMON SCARLET:

Cryogonal appear during cold seasons. It is said that people and Pokémon who die on snowy mountains are reborn into these Pokémon.

POKÉMON VIOLET:

Cryogonal uses its chains of ice to constrict its opponents and then flash-freezes them where they stand.

Does not evolve.

CUBCHOO

CHILL POKÉMON

TYPE: ICE

How to Say It: cub-CHOO
Imperial Height: 1'08"
Metric Height: 0.5 m
Imperial Weight: 18.7 lbs.
Metric Weight: 8.5 kg
Gender: ♂♀
Abilities: Snow Cloak, Slush Rush
Weaknesses: Fire, Fighting, Rock, Steel

POKÉMON SCARLET:

Many of this species can be found along the shorelines of cold regions. If a Cubchoo lacks dangling snot, there's a chance it is sick.

POKÉMON VIOLET:

When Cubchoo starts sneezing, watch out! If it spatters you with its frosty snot, you'll get frostbite.

Cubchoo → **Beartic**

CUFANT

COPPERDERM POKÉMON

How to Say It: KYOO-funt
Imperial Height: 3'11"
Metric Height: 1.2 m
Imperial Weight: 220.5 lbs.
Metric Weight: 100.0 kg
Gender: ♂♀
Abilities: Sheer Force
Weaknesses: Fire, Fighting, Ground

TYPE: STEEL

POKÉMON SCARLET:

Using the pointy tip of its trunk, it carves off chunks of hard rocks to eat. It is very docile and helps people with physical labor.

POKÉMON VIOLET:

Cufant can lift loads weighing five tons. In the mornings, it heads into caves with its herd, in search of the ore on which these Pokémon feed.

Cufant → Copperajah

CYCLIZAR

MOUNT POKÉMON

TYPE: DRAGON-NORMAL

How to Say It: SYE-clih-zahr
Imperial Height: 5'03"
Metric Height: 1.6 m
Imperial Weight: 138.9 lbs.
Metric Weight: 63.0 kg
Gender: ♂♀
Abilities: Shed Skin
Weaknesses: Fairy, Ice, Fighting, Dragon

POKÉMON SCARLET:

Apparently Cyclizar has been allowing people to ride on its back since ancient times. Depictions of this have been found in 10,000-year-old murals.

POKÉMON VIOLET:

It can sprint at over 70 mph while carrying a human. The rider's body heat warms Cyclizar's back and lifts the Pokémon's spirit.

Does not evolve.

DACHSBUN

DOG POKÉMON

How to Say It: DAHKS-buhn
Imperial Height: 1'08"
Metric Height: 0.5 m
Imperial Weight: 32.8 lbs.
Metric Weight: 14.9 kg
Gender: ♂ ♀
Abilities: Well-Baked Body
Weaknesses: Steel, Poison

**TYPE:
FAIRY**

POKÉMON SCARLET:

The pleasant aroma that emanates from this Pokémon's body helps wheat grow, so Dachsbun has been treasured by farming villages.

POKÉMON VIOLET:

The surface of this Pokémon's skin hardens when exposed to intense heat, and its body has an appetizing aroma.

Fidough → Dachsbun

DEDENNE

ANTENNA POKÉMON

How to Say It: deh-DEN-nay
Imperial Height: 0'08"
Metric Height: 0.2 m
Imperial Weight: 4.9 lbs.
Metric Weight: 2.2 kg
Gender: ♂ ♀
Abilities: Pickup, Cheek Pouch
Weaknesses: Poison, Ground

**TYPE:
ELECTRIC-
FAIRY**

POKÉMON SCARLET:

It's small and its electricity-generating organ is not fully developed, so it uses its tail to absorb electricity from people's homes and charge itself.

POKÉMON VIOLET:

Dedenne emit electrical waves from the whiskers on their cheeks to communicate with each other. When low on electricity, they curl up and sleep.

Does not evolve.

DEERLING

SEASON POKÉMON

How to Say It: DEER-ling
Imperial Height: 2'00"
Metric Height: 0.6 m
Imperial Weight: 43.0 lbs.
Metric Weight: 19.5 kg
Gender: ♂♀
Abilities: Chlorophyll, Sap Sipper
Weaknesses: Fire, Flying, Fighting, Ice, Poison, Bug

**TYPE:
NORMAL-
GRASS**

SUMMER FORM

AUTUMN FORM

SPRING FORM

WINTER FORM

POKÉMON SCARLET:

Deerling have different scents depending on the season. In early spring, these Pokémon give off a delicate, sweet, and calming scent.

POKÉMON VIOLET:

Despite Deerling's adorable appearance, farmers consider it a nuisance since it loves plant shoots and will eat them all up.

Deerling ➡ **Sawsbuck**

DEINO

IRATE POKÉMON

**TYPE:
DARK-
DRAGON**

How to Say It: DY-noh
Imperial Height: 2'07"
Metric Height: 0.8 m
Imperial Weight: 38.1 lbs.
Metric Weight: 17.3 kg
Gender: ♂♀
Abilities: Hustle
Weaknesses: Ice, Fighting, Bug, Dragon, Fairy

POKÉMON SCARLET:

It can't see, so its first approach to examining things is to bite them. You will be covered in wounds until a Deino warms up to you.

POKÉMON VIOLET:

It nests deep inside a cave. Food there is scarce, so Deino will sink its teeth into anything that moves and attempt to eat it.

Deino ➡ **Zweilous** ➡ **Hydreigon**

DELIBIRD

DELIVERY POKÉMON

TYPE:
ICE-
FLYING

How to Say It: DELL-ee-bird
Imperial Height: 2'11"
Metric Height: 0.9 m
Imperial Weight: 35.3
Metric Weight: 16.0 kg
Gender: ♂ ♀
Abilities: Vital Spirit, Hustle
Weaknesses: Rock, Electric, Fire, Steel

POKÉMON SCARLET:
It carries food all day long. There are tales about lost people who were saved by the food it had.

POKÉMON VIOLET:
It always carries its food with it, wherever it goes. If attacked, it throws its food at the opponent.

Does not evolve.

DIGLETT

MOLE POKÉMON

How to Say It: DIG-let
Imperial Height: 0'08"
Metric Height: 0.2 m
Imperial Weight: 1.8 lbs.
Metric Weight: 0.8 kg
Gender: ♂ ♀
Abilities: Sand Veil, Arena Trap
Weaknesses: Grass, Ice, Water

TYPE:
GROUND

POKÉMON SCARLET:
It lives about one yard underground, where it feeds on plant roots. It sometimes appears aboveground.

POKÉMON VIOLET:
Its skin is very thin. If it is exposed to light, its blood heats up, causing it to grow weak.

Diglett   Dugtrio

DITTO

TRANSFORM POKÉMON

How to Say It: DIT-toe
Imperial Height: 1'00"
Metric Height: 0.3 m
Imperial Weight: 8.8 lbs.
Metric Weight: 4.0 kg
Gender: Unknown
Abilities: Limber
Weaknesses: Fighting

TYPE:
NORMAL

POKÉMON SCARLET:

Its transformation ability is perfect. However, if made to laugh, it can't maintain its disguise.

POKÉMON VIOLET:

It can freely recombine its own cellular structure to transform into other life-forms.

Does not evolve.

DOLLIV

OLIVE POKÉMON

How to Say It: DAH-liv
Imperial Height: 2'00"
Metric Height: 0.6 m
Imperial Weight: 26.2 lbs.
Metric Weight: 11.9 kg
Gender: ♂♀
Abilities: Early Bird
Weaknesses: Ice, Fire, Flying, Poison, Fighting, Bug

TYPE:
GRASS-NORMAL

POKÉMON SCARLET:

Dolliv shares its tasty, fresh-scented oil with others. This species has coexisted with humans since times long gone.

POKÉMON VIOLET:

It basks in the sun to its heart's content until the fruits on its head ripen. After that, Dolliv departs from human settlements and goes on a journey.

Smoliv → Dolliv → Arboliva

DONDOZO

BIG CATFISH POKÉMON

TYPE:

WATER

How to Say It: DAHN-DOH-zoh
Imperial Height: 39'04"
Metric Height: 12.0 m
Imperial Weight: 485.0 lbs.
Metric Weight: 222.0 kg
Gender: ♂♀
Abilities: Oblivious, Unaware
Weaknesses: Grass, Electric

POKÉMON SCARLET:

This Pokémon is a glutton, but it's bad at getting food. It teams up with a Tatsugiri to catch prey.

POKÉMON VIOLET:

It treats Tatsugiri like its boss and follows it loyally. Though powerful, Dondozo is apparently not very smart.

Does not evolve.

DONPHAN

ARMOR POKÉMON

TYPE:

GROUND

How to Say It: DON-fan
Imperial Height: 3'07"
Metric Height: 1.1 m
Imperial Weight: 264.6 lbs.
Metric Weight: 120.0 kg
Gender: ♂♀
Abilities: Sturdy
Weaknesses: Water, Grass, Ice

POKÉMON SCARLET:

Donphan is covered in tough hide, so even being hit by a car won't faze this Pokémon. However, it is extremely susceptible to rain.

POKÉMON VIOLET:

Donphan is normally a calm Pokémon, but once it is enraged, it will curl its body into a ball and charge at you while rolling.

Phanpy   Donphan

55

DRAGALGE

MOCK KELP POKÉMON

How to Say It: druh-GAL-jee
Imperial Height: 5'11"
Metric Height: 1.8 m
Imperial Weight: 179.7 lbs.
Metric Weight: 81.5 kg
Gender: ♂♀
Abilities: Poison Point, Poison Touch
Weaknesses: Psychic, Ground, Ice, Dragon

**TYPE:
POISON-
DRAGON**

POKÉMON SCARLET:

Using a liquid poison, Dragalge indiscriminately attacks anything that wanders into its territory. This poison can corrode the undersides of boats.

POKÉMON VIOLET:

Since Finizen is the better swimmer, Dragalge will approach it under the cover of seaweed, then immobilize it with a poisonous attack.

Skrelp → Dragalge

DRAGAPULT

STEALTH POKÉMON

How to Say It: DRAG-uh-pult
Imperial Height: 9'10"
Metric Height: 3.0 m
Imperial Weight: 110.2 lbs.
Metric Weight: 50.0 kg
Gender: ♂♀
Abilities: Clear Body, Infiltrator
Weaknesses: Ghost, Dark, Fairy, Ice, Dragon

**TYPE:
DRAGON-
GHOST**

POKÉMON SCARLET:

Dragapult can make its whole body transparent by clearing its mind and focusing. Even the Dreepy in Dragapult's horns become invisible.

POKÉMON VIOLET:

The fastest Dragapult of the group is always surrounded by Dreepy that want to fly at sonic speed.

Dreepy → Drakloak → Dragapult

DRAGONAIR

DRAGON POKÉMON

TYPE:
DRAGON

How to Say It: DRAG-gon-AIR
Imperial Height: 13'01"
Metric Height: 4.0 m
Imperial Weight: 36.4 lbs.
Metric Weight: 16.5 kg
Gender: ♂♀
Abilities: Shed Skin
Weaknesses: Fairy, ice, Dragon

POKÉMON SCARLET:
They say that if it emits an aura from its whole body, the weather will begin to change instantly.

POKÉMON VIOLET:
It is called the divine Pokémon. When its entire body brightens slightly, the weather changes.

Dratini → Dragonair → Dragonite

DRAGONITE

DRAGON POKÉMON

How to Say It: DRAG-gon-ite
Imperial Height: 7'03"
Metric Height: 2.2 m
Imperial Weight: 463.0 lbs.
Metric Weight: 210.0 kg
Gender: ♂♀
Abilities: Inner Focus
Weaknesses: Fairy, Dragon, Ice, Rock

TYPE:
DRAGON-FLYING

POKÉMON SCARLET:
It is said that somewhere in the ocean lies an island where these gather. Only they live there.

POKÉMON VIOLET:
It can fly in spite of its big and bulky physique. It circles the globe in just 16 hours.

Dratini → Dragonair → Dragonite

DRAKLOAK

CARETAKER POKÉMON

How to Say It: DRAK-klohk
Imperial Height: 4'07"
Metric Height: 1.4 m
Imperial Weight: 24.3 lbs.
Metric Weight: 11.0 kg
Gender: ♂♀
Abilities: Clear Body, Infiltrator
Weaknesses: Ghost, Dark, Fairy, Ice, Dragon

TYPE:
DRAGON-GHOST

POKÉMON SCARLET:

This Pokémon flies around at over 120 miles per hour. If a Drakloak is defeated in a battle, its Dreepy will wander off without a second thought.

POKÉMON VIOLET:

This Pokémon stores up energy in its lungs, then shoots it out. It takes care of Dreepy and battles alongside them until they're all grown up.

Dreepy → **Drakloak** → **Dragapult**

DRATINI

DRAGON POKÉMON

TYPE:
DRAGON

How to Say It: dra-TEE-nee
Imperial Height: 5'11"
Metric Height: 1.8 m
Imperial Weight: 7.3 lbs.
Metric Weight: 3.3 kg
Gender: ♂♀
Abilities: Shed Skin
Weaknesses: Fairy, Ice, Dragon

POKÉMON SCARLET:

It sheds many layers of skin as it grows larger. During this process, it is protected by a rapid waterfall.

POKÉMON VIOLET:

It is born large to start with. It repeatedly sheds its skin as it steadily grows longer.

Dratini → **Dragonair** → **Dragonite**

DREDNAW

BITE POKÉMON

TYPE:
WATER-ROCK

How to Say It: DRED-naw
Imperial Height: 3'03"
Metric Height: 1.0 m
Imperial Weight: 254.6 lbs.
Metric Weight: 115.5 kg
Gender: ♂♀
Abilities: Shell Armor, Strong Jaw
Weaknesses: Grass, Electric, Fighting, Ground

POKÉMON SCARLET:

Its massive, jagged teeth can crush a boulder in a single bite. This Pokémon has an extremely vicious disposition.

POKÉMON VIOLET:

Drednaw lurks along the shoreline. When prey come to drink water, Drednaw stretches its neck out and chomps down on them.

Chewtle → Drednaw

DREEPY

LINGERING POKÉMON

TYPE:
DRAGON-GHOST

How to Say It: DREE-pee
Imperial Height: 1'08"
Metric Height: 0.5 m
Imperial Weight: 4.4 lbs.
Metric Weight: 2.0 kg
Gender: ♂♀
Abilities: Clear Body, Infiltrator
Weaknesses: Ghost, Dark, Fairy, Ice, Dragon

POKÉMON SCARLET:

In the evening, groups of Dreepy will fly at high speeds over the ocean and poke at Pokémon in the water for fun.

POKÉMON VIOLET:

It has a habit of biting at Clauncher even though it doesn't feed on them. This is said to be vestigial behavior from when Dreepy was alive.

Dreepy → Drakloak → Dragapult

DRIFBLIM

BLIMP POKÉMON

How to Say It: DRIFF-blim
Imperial Height: 3'11"
Metric Height: 1.2 m
Imperial Weight: 33.1 lbs.
Metric Weight: 15.0 kg
Gender: ♂♀
Abilities: Aftermath, Unburden
Weaknesses: Ghost, Dark, Electric, Ice, Rock

**TYPE:
GHOST-
FLYING**

POKÉMON SCARLET:

It can generate and release gas within its body. That's how it can control the altitude of its drift.

POKÉMON VIOLET:

They carry people and Pokémon, but the wind can catch them, so there can't be a fixed destination.

Drifloon   Drifblim

DRIFLOON

BALLOON POKÉMON

**TYPE:
GHOST-
FLYING**

How to Say It: DRIFF-loon
Imperial Height: 1'04"
Metric Height: 0.4 m
Imperial Weight: 2.6 lbs.
Metric Weight: 1.2 kg
Gender: ♂♀
Abilities: Aftermath, Unburden
Weaknesses: Ghost, Dark, Electric, Ice, Rock

POKÉMON SCARLET:

It is whispered that any child who mistakes Drifloon for a balloon and holds on to it could wind up missing.

POKÉMON VIOLET:

Because of the way it floats aimlessly, an old folktale calls it a "signpost for wandering spirits."

Drifloon   Drifblim

DROWZEE

HYPNOSIS POKÉMON

HYPNOSIS POKÉMON

TYPE:

PSYCHIC

How to Say It: DROW-zee
Imperial Height: 3'03"
Metric Height: 1.0 m
Imperial Weight: 71.4 lbs.
Metric Weight: 32.4 kg
Gender: ♂♀
Abilities: Insomnia, Forewarn
Weaknesses: Ghost, Dark, Bug

POKÉMON SCARLET:

It remembers every dream it eats. It rarely eats the dreams of adults because children's are much tastier.

POKÉMON VIOLET:

When it twitches its nose, it can tell where someone is sleeping and what that person is dreaming about.

Drowzee → Hypno

DUDUNSPARCE

LAND SNAKE POKÉMON

How to Say It: duh-DUHN-sparse
Imperial Height: 11'10"
Metric Height: 3.6 m
Imperial Weight: 86.4 lbs.
Metric Weight: 39.2 kg
Gender: ♂♀
Abilities: Run Away, Serene Grace
Weaknesses: Fighting

TYPE:

NORMAL

POKÉMON SCARLET:

This Pokémon uses its hard tail to make its nest by boring holes into bedrock deep underground. The nest can reach lengths of over six miles.

POKÉMON VIOLET:

It drives enemies out of its nest by sucking in enough air to fill its long, narrow lungs, then releasing the air in an intense blast.

Dunsparce → Dudunsparce

DUGTRIO

MOLE POKÉMON

How to Say It: DUG-TREE-oh
Imperial Height: 2'04"
Metric Height: 0.7 m
Imperial Weight: 73.4 lbs.
Metric Weight: 33.3 kg
Gender: ♂♀
Abilities: Sand Veil, Arena Trap
Weaknesses: Water, Grass, Ice

TYPE: GROUND

POKÉMON SCARLET:
Its three heads bob separately up and down to loosen the soil nearby, making it easier for it to burrow.

POKÉMON VIOLET:
In battle, it digs through the ground and strikes the unsuspecting foe from an unexpected direction.

Diglett   Dugtrio

DUNSPARCE

LAND SNAKE POKÉMON

TYPE: NORMAL

How to Say It: DUN-sparce
Imperial Height: 4'11"
Metric Height: 1.5 m
Imperial Weight: 30.9 lbs.
Metric Weight: 14.0 kg
Gender: ♂♀
Abilities: Run Away, Serene Grace
Weaknesses: Fighting

POKÉMON SCARLET:
It creates mazes in dark locations. When spotted, it flees into the ground by digging with its tail.

POKÉMON VIOLET:
If spotted, it escapes by burrowing with its tail. It can float just slightly using its wings.

Dunsparce   Dudunsparce

EELEKTRIK

ELEFISH POKÉMON

TYPE: ELECTRIC

How to Say It: ee-LEK-trik
Imperial Height: 3'11"
Metric Height: 1.2 m
Imperial Weight: 48.5 lbs.
Metric Weight: 22.0 kg
Gender: ♂♀
Abilities: Levitate
Weaknesses: Ground

POKÉMON SCARLET:

They coil around foes and shock them with electricity-generating organs that seem simply to be circular patterns.

POKÉMON VIOLET:

These Pokémon have a big appetite. When they spot their prey, they attack it and paralyze it with electricity.

Tynamo → Eelektrik → Eelektross

EELEKTROSS

ELEFISH POKÉMON

TYPE: ELECTRIC

How to Say It: ee-LEK-trahs
Imperial Height: 6'11"
Metric Height: 2.1 m
Imperial Weight: 177.5 lbs.
Metric Weight: 80.5 kg
Gender: ♂♀
Abilities: Levitate
Weaknesses: Ground

POKÉMON SCARLET:

They crawl out of the ocean using their arms. They will attack prey onshore and immediately drag it into the ocean.

POKÉMON VIOLET:

It latches on to prey with its sucker mouth, sinking in its fangs and shocking the prey with powerful electricity.

Tynamo → Eelektrik → Eelektross

EEVEE

EVOLUTION POKÉMON

How to Say It: EE-vee
Imperial Height: 1'00"
Metric Height: 0.3 m
Imperial Weight: 14.3 lbs.
Metric Weight: 6.5 kg
Gender: ♂♀
Abilities: Run Away, Adaptability
Weaknesses: Fighting

TYPE: NORMAL

POKÉMON SCARLET:

Its ability to evolve into many forms allows it to adapt smoothly and perfectly to any environment.

POKÉMON VIOLET:

Its genetic code is irregular. It may mutate if it is exposed to radiation from element stones.

EISCUE

PENGUIN POKÉMON

TYPE: ICE

How to Say It: ICE-kyoo
Imperial Height: 4'07"
Metric Height: 1.4 m
Imperial Weight: 196.2 lbs.
Metric Weight: 89.0 kg
Gender: ♂♀
Abilities: Ice Face
Weaknesses: Fire, Steel, Fighting, Rock

POKÉMON SCARLET:

On hot days, these Pokémon press their ice cube heads together and pass the time cooling each other down.

POKÉMON VIOLET:

If you lick the ice covering its face, you'll find it has a faintly salty taste. This species rode here on ocean currents from a cold, faraway land.

Does not evolve.

ELECTRODE

BALL POKÉMON

TYPE:
ELECTRIC

How to Say It: ee-LECK-trode
Imperial Height: 3'11"
Metric Height: 1.2 m
Imperial Weight: 146.8 lbs.
Metric Weight: 66.6 kg
Gender: ♂♀
Abilities: Static, Soundproof
Weaknesses: Ground

POKÉMON SCARLET:

The more energy it charges up, the faster it gets. But this also makes it more likely to explode.

POKÉMON VIOLET:

It explodes in response to even minor stimuli. It is feared, with the nickname of the Bomb Ball.

Voltorb → **Electrode**

ESPATHRA

OSTRICH POKÉMON

How to Say It: ess-PATH-ruh
Imperial Height: 6'03"
Metric Height: 1.9 m
Imperial Weight: 198.4 lbs.
Metric Weight: 90.0 kg
Gender: ♂♀
Abilities: Frisk, Opportunist
Weaknesses: Ghost, Dark, Bug

TYPE:
PSYCHIC

POKÉMON SCARLET:

It immobilizes opponents by bathing them in psychic power from its large eyes. Despite its appearance, it has a vicious temperament.

POKÉMON VIOLET:

It emits psychic power from the gaps between its multicolored frills and sprints at speeds greater than 120 mph.

Flittle → **Espathra**

ESPEON

SUN POKÉMON

How to Say It: ESS-pee-on
Imperial Height: 2'11"
Metric Height: 0.9 m
Imperial Weight: 58.4 lbs.
Metric Weight: 26.5 kg
Gender: ♂♀
Abilities: Synchronize
Weaknesses: Ghost, Dark, Bug

TYPE:
PSYCHIC

POKÉMON SCARLET:

The tip of its forked tail quivers when it is predicting its opponent's next move.

POKÉMON VIOLET:

It uses the fine hair that covers its body to sense air currents and predict its enemy's actions.

Eevee ⇨ Espeon

FALINKS

FORMATION POKÉMON

How to Say It: FAY-links
Imperial Height: 9'10"
Metric Height: 3.0 m
Imperial Weight: 136.7 lbs.
Metric Weight: 62.0 kg
Gender: Unknown
Abilities: Battle Armor
Weaknesses: Psychic, Flying, Fairy

TYPE:
FIGHTING

POKÉMON SCARLET:

The brass, which is the one that stands at the front and issues orders, is the strongest and smartest of the six.

POKÉMON VIOLET:

The leader, known as the brass, uses its extendible horn to issue orders to the others when it's time to change formation.

Does not evolve.

FARIGIRAF

LONG NECK POKÉMON

TYPE: NORMAL-PSYCHIC

How to Say It: fuh-RIG-uh-raff
Imperial Height: 10'06"
Metric Height: 3.2 m
Imperial Weight: 352.7 lbs.
Metric Weight: 160.0 kg
Gender: ♂♀
Abilities: Cud Chew, Armor Tail
Weaknesses: Dark, Bug

POKÉMON SCARLET:

Now that the brain waves from the head and tail are synced up, the psychic power of this Pokémon is ten times stronger than Girafarig's.

POKÉMON VIOLET:

The hardened head from the tail protects the head of the main body as Farigiraf whips its long neck around to headbutt enemies.

Girafarig → Farigiraf

FIDOUGH

PUPPY POKÉMON

How to Say It: FEYE-doh
Imperial Height: 1'00"
Metric Height: 0.3 m
Imperial Weight: 24.0 lbs.
Metric Weight: 10.9 kg
Gender: ♂♀
Abilities: Own Tempo
Weaknesses: Steel, Poison

TYPE: FAIRY

POKÉMON SCARLET:

This Pokémon is smooth and moist to the touch. Yeast in Fidough's breath induces fermentation in the Pokémon's vicinity.

POKÉMON VIOLET:

The yeast in Fidough's breath is useful for cooking, so this Pokémon has been protected by people since long ago.

Fidough → Dachsbun

FINIZEN

DOLPHIN POKÉMON

How to Say It: FIN-uh-zin
Imperial Height: 4'03"
Metric Height: 1.3 m
Imperial Weight: 132.7 lbs.
Metric Weight: 60.2 kg
Gender: ♂♀
Abilities: Water Veil
Weaknesses: Grass, Electric

TYPE:
WATER

POKÉMON SCARLET:

It likes playing with others of its kind using the water ring on its tail. It uses ultrasonic waves to sense the emotions of other living creatures.

POKÉMON VIOLET:

Its water ring is made from seawater mixed with a sticky fluid that Finizen secretes from its blowhole.

Finizen   Palafin

FINNEON

WING FISH POKÉMON

How to Say It: FINN-ee-on
Imperial Height: 1'04"
Metric Height: 0.4 m
Imperial Weight: 15.4 lbs.
Metric Weight: 7.0 kg
Gender: ♂♀
Abilities: Swift Swim, Storm Drain
Weaknesses: Grass, Electric

TYPE:
WATER

POKÉMON SCARLET:

The line running down its side can store sunlight. It shines vividly at night.

POKÉMON VIOLET:

It absorbs sunlight with the pink areas of its skin, which then shine. This appears to be a form of camouflage.

Finneon   Lumineon

FLAAFFY

WOOL POKÉMON

TYPE:
ELECTRIC

How to Say It: FLAF-fee
Imperial Height: 2'07"
Metric Height: 0.8 m
Imperial Weight: 29.3 lbs.
Metric Weight: 13.3 kg
Gender: ♂ ♀
Abilities: Static
Weaknesses: Ground

POKÉMON SCARLET:

As a result of storing too much electricity, it developed patches where even downy wool won't grow.

POKÉMON VIOLET:

Because of its rubbery, electricity-resistant skin, it can store lots of electricity in its fur.

Mareep → **Flaaffy** → **Ampharos**

FLABÉBÉ

SINGLE BLOOM POKÉMON

How to Say It: flah-BAY-BAY
Imperial Height: 0'04"
Metric Height: 0.1 m
Imperial Weight: 0.2 lbs.
Metric Weight: 0.1 kg
Gender: ♀
Abilities: Flower Veil
Weaknesses: Steel, Poison

TYPE:
FAIRY

POKÉMON SCARLET:

This Pokémon can draw forth the power hidden within blooming wildflowers. It is particularly fond of red flowers.

POKÉMON VIOLET:

This Flabébé rides a red flower. Immediately after birth, this Pokémon begins flying around in search of a flower it likes.

Flabébé → **Floette** → **Florges**

69

FLAMIGO

How to Say It: fluh-MEE-goh
Imperial Height: 5'03"
Metric Height: 1.6 m
Imperial Weight: 81.6 lbs.
Metric Weight: 37.0 kg
Gender: ♂♀
Abilities: Tangled Feet, Scrappy
Weaknesses: Psychic, Flying, Fairy, Electric, Ice

TYPE:
FLYING-FIGHTING

POKÉMON SCARLET:

This Pokémon apparently ties the base of its neck into a knot so that energy stored in its belly does not escape from its beak.

POKÉMON VIOLET:

Thanks to a behavior of theirs known as "synchronizing," an entire flock of these Pokémon can attack simultaneously in perfect harmony.

Does not evolve.

FLAPPLE

APPLE WING POKÉMON

How to Say It: FLAP-puhl
Imperial Height: 1'00"
Metric Height: 0.3 m
Imperial Weight: 2.2 lbs.
Metric Weight: 1.0 kg
Gender: ♂♀
Abilities: Ripen, Gluttony
Weaknesses: Flying, Ice, Dragon, Poison, Fairy, Bug

TYPE:
GRASS-DRAGON

POKÉMON SCARLET:

It flutters around while seeking an opening in the opponent's guard, then attacks by spitting acidic liquid strong enough to melt metal.

POKÉMON VIOLET:

It uses its own body fluid to repair its apple. Strong Flapple that have won many battles have apples that are clay colored all over.

Applin → Appletun → Flapple

FLAREON

FLAME POKÉMON

How to Say It: FLAIR-ee-on
Imperial Height: 2'11"
Metric Height: 0.9 m
Imperial Weight: 55.1 lbs.
Metric Weight: 25.0 kg
Gender: ♂♀
Abilities: Flash Fire
Weaknesses: Water, Ground, Rock

TYPE:
FIRE

POKÉMON SCARLET:
Inhaled air is carried to its flame sac, heated, and exhaled as fire that reaches over 3,000 degrees Fahrenheit.

POKÉMON VIOLET:
It fluffs out its fur collar to cool down its body temperature, which can reach 1,650 degrees Fahrenheit.

Eevee → Flareon

FLETCHINDER

EMBER POKÉMON

How to Say It: FLETCH-in-der
Imperial Height: 2'04"
Metric Height: 0.7 m
Imperial Weight: 35.3 lbs.
Metric Weight: 16.0 kg
Gender: ♂♀
Abilities: Flame Body
Weaknesses: Water, Electric, Rock

TYPE:
FIRE-
FLYING

POKÉMON SCARLET:
Fletchinder scatters embers in tall grass where bug Pokémon might be hiding and then catches them as they come leaping out.

POKÉMON VIOLET:
Its territory has a radius of just over a mile. If any bird Pokémon should enter, it will show them no mercy.

Fletchling → Fletchinder → Talonflame

FLETCHLING

TINY ROBIN POKÉMON

How to Say It: FLETCH-ling
Imperial Height: 1'00"
Metric Height: 0.3 m
Imperial Weight: 3.7 lbs.
Metric Weight: 1.7 kg
Gender: ♂♀
Abilities: Big Pecks
Weaknesses: Electric, Ice, Rock

TYPE:
NORMAL-FLYING

POKÉMON SCARLET:

This Pokémon is normally calm, but once it enters battle, its hormonal balance changes and it becomes aggressive.

POKÉMON VIOLET:

Fletchling can be found in both rural and urban areas. They once had a huge territorial dispute with Squawkabilly. Fights broke out all over town.

Fletchling → Fletchinder → Talonflame

FLITTLE

FRILL POKÉMON

TYPE:
PSYCHIC

How to Say It: FLIT-ull
Imperial Height: 0'08"
Metric Height: 0.2 m
Imperial Weight: 3.3 lbs.
Metric Weight: 1.5 kg
Gender: ♂♀
Abilities: Frisk, Anticipation
Weaknesses: Ghost, Dark, Bug

POKÉMON SCARLET:

Flittle's toes levitate about half an inch above the ground because of the psychic power emitted from the frills on the Pokémon's belly.

POKÉMON VIOLET:

It spends its time running around wastelands. If anyone steals its beloved berries, it will chase them down and exact its revenge.

Flittle → Espathra

FLOATZEL

SEA WEASEL POKÉMON

TYPE:
WATER

How to Say It: FLOAT-zul
Imperial Height: 3'07"
Metric Height: 1.1 m
Imperial Weight: 73.9 lbs.
Metric Weight: 33.5 kg
Gender: ♂♀
Abilities: Swift Swim
Weaknesses: Grass, Electric

POKÉMON SCARLET:

With its flotation sac inflated, it can carry people on its back. It deflates the sac before it dives.

POKÉMON VIOLET:

It is a common sight around fishing ports. It is known to rescue people and help fishers carry what they caught.

Buizel → Floatzel

FLOETTE

SINGLE BLOOM POKÉMON

TYPE:
FAIRY

How to Say It: floh-ET
Imperial Height: 0'08"
Metric Height: 0.2 m
Imperial Weight: 2.0 lbs.
Metric Weight: 0.9 kg
Gender: ♀
Abilities: Flower Veil
Weaknesses: Steel, Poison

POKÉMON SCARLET:

This Pokémon draws forth what power is left in withered flowers to make them healthy again. It holds a red flower.

POKÉMON VIOLET:

This Pokémon uses red wavelengths of light to pour its own energy into flowers and draw forth their latent potential.

Flabébé → Floette → Florges

FLORAGATO

GRASS CAT POKÉMON

How to Say It: FLOR-uh-GAH-toh
Imperial Height: 2'11"
Metric Height: 0.9 m
Imperial Weight: 26.9 lbs.
Metric Weight: 12.2 kg
Gender: ♂♀
Abilities: Overgrow
Weaknesses: Fire, Flying, Ice, Poison, Bug

TYPE:
GRASS

POKÉMON SCARLET:
Floragato deftly wields the vine hidden beneath its long fur, slamming the hard flower bud against its opponents.

POKÉMON VIOLET:
The hardness of Floragato's fur depends on the Pokémon's mood. When Floragato is prepared to battle, its fur becomes pointed and needle sharp.

Sprigatito → **Floragato** → **Meowscarada**

FLORGES

GARDEN POKÉMON

How to Say It: FLORE-jess
Imperial Height: 3'07"
Metric Height: 1.1 m
Imperial Weight: 22.0 lbs.
Metric Weight: 10.0 kg
Gender: ♀
Abilities: Flower Veil
Weaknesses: Steel, Poison

TYPE:
FAIRY

POKÉMON SCARLET:
This Pokémon creates an impressive flower garden in its territory. It draws forth the power of the red flowers around its neck.

POKÉMON VIOLET:
They say that flower gardens created by Florges are constantly showered with a power that can heal both body and spirit.

Flabébé → **Floette** → **Florges**

FLUTTER MANE

PARADOX POKÉMON

How to Say It: FLUH-ter mane
Imperial Height: 4'07"
Metric Height: 1.4 m
Imperial Weight: 8.8 lbs.
Metric Weight: 4.0 kg
Gender: Unknown
Abilities: Protosynthesis
Weaknesses: Ghost, Steel

TYPE:
GHOST-FAIRY

POKÉMON SCARLET:

This Pokémon has characteristics similar to those of Flutter Mane, a creature mentioned in a certain book.

POKÉMON VIOLET:

It has similar features to a ghostly pterosaur that was covered in a paranormal magazine, but the two have little else in common.

Does not evolve.

FOMANTIS

SICKLE GRASS POKÉMON

How to Say It: fo-MAN-tis
Imperial Height: 1'00"
Metric Height: 0.3 m
Imperial Weight: 3.3 lbs.
Metric Weight: 1.5 kg
Gender: ♂♀
Abilities: Leaf Guard
Weaknesses: Fire, Flying, Ice, Poison, Bug

TYPE:
GRASS

POKÉMON SCARLET:

Fomantis hates having its naps interrupted. It fires off beams using energy it gathers by bathing in the sun.

POKÉMON VIOLET:

Many Trainers give their Fomantis their own flowerpots so they can sunbathe in peace and quiet.

Fomantis → Lurantis

FOONGUS

MUSHROOM POKÉMON

How to Say It: FOON-gus
Imperial Height: 0'08"
Metric Height: 0.2 m
Imperial Weight: 2.2 lbs.
Metric Weight: 1.0 kg
Gender: ♂♀
Abilities: Effect Spore
Weaknesses: Fire, Psychic, Flying, Ice

TYPE: GRASS-POISON

POKÉMON SCARLET:

There is a theory that the developer of the modern-day Poké Ball really liked Foongus, but this has not been confirmed.

POKÉMON VIOLET:

This Pokémon prefers damp places. It spurts out poison spores to repel approaching enemies.

Foongus → Amoonguss

FORRETRESS

BAGWORM POKÉMON

How to Say It: FOR-it-tress
Imperial Height: 3'11"
Metric Height: 1.2 m
Imperial Weight: 277.3 lbs.
Metric Weight: 125.8 kg
Gender: ♂♀
Abilities: Sturdy
Weaknesses: Fire

TYPE: BUG-STEEL

POKÉMON SCARLET:

It's usually found hanging on to a fat tree trunk. It shoots out bits of its shell when it sees action.

POKÉMON VIOLET:

Its entire body is shielded by a steel-hard shell. What lurks inside this shell is a total mystery.

Pineco → Forretress

FRAXURE

AXE JAW POKÉMON

**TYPE:
DRAGON**

How to Say It: FRAK-shur
Imperial Height: 3'03"
Metric Height: 1.0 m
Imperial Weight: 79.4 lbs.
Metric Weight: 36.0 kg
Gender: ♂♀
Abilities: Rivalry, Mold Breaker
Weaknesses: Fairy, Ice, Dragon

POKÉMON SCARLET:
Because its tusks don't grow back once they break, this Pokémon apparently won't use them unless truly necessary.

POKÉMON VIOLET:
Fraxure uses its thick tusks to neatly cut prey into two portions—one to eat now and one to save for later.

Axew → Fraxure → Haxorus

FRIGIBAX

ICE FIN POKÉMON

How to Say It: FRI-juh-baks
Imperial Height: 1'08"
Metric Height: 0.5 m
Imperial Weight: 37.5 lbs.
Metric Weight: 17.0 kg
Gender: ♂♀
Abilities: Thermal Exchange
Weaknesses: Steel, Fairy, Rock, Fighting, Dragon

**TYPE:
DRAGON-
ICE**

POKÉMON SCARLET:
Frigibax absorbs heat through its dorsal fin and converts the heat into ice energy. The higher the temperature, the more energy Frigibax stores.

POKÉMON VIOLET:
This Pokémon lives in forests and craggy areas. Using the power of its dorsal fin, it cools the inside of its nest like a refrigerator.

Frigibax → Arctibax → Baxcalibur

FROSLASS

SNOW LAND POKÉMON

How to Say It: FROS-lass
Imperial Height: 4'03"
Metric Height: 1.3 m
Imperial Weight: 58.6 lbs.
Metric Weight: 26.6 kg
Gender: ♀
Abilities: Snow Cloak
Weaknesses: Steel, Ghost, Fire, Dark, Rock

TYPE:
ICE-
GHOST

POKÉMON SCARLET:

When it finds humans or Pokémon it likes, it freezes them and takes them to its chilly den, where they become decorations.

POKÉMON VIOLET:

It freezes prey by blowing its –58 degree Fahrenheit breath. It is said to then secretly display its prey.

Snorunt   Froslass

FROSMOTH

FROST MOTH POKÉMON

TYPE:
ICE-
BUG

How to Say It: FRAHS-mahth
Imperial Height: 4'03"
Metric Height: 1.3 m
Imperial Weight: 92.6 lbs.
Metric Weight: 42.0 kg
Gender: ♂ ♀
Abilities: Shield Dust
Weaknesses: Fire, Steel, Flying, Rock

POKÉMON SCARLET:

Frosmoth senses air currents with its antennae. It sends its scales drifting on frigid air, making them fall like snow.

POKÉMON VIOLET:

It causes blizzards as it flies around with its huge, chill-emanating wings. Clean meltwater is its favorite thing to drink.

Snom   Frosmoth

FUECOCO

FIRE CROC POKÉMON

TYPE:
FIRE

How to Say It: fwey-KO-ko
Imperial Height: 1'04"
Metric Height: 0.4 m
Imperial Weight: 21.6 lbs.
Metric Weight: 9.8 kg
Gender: ♂♀
Abilities: Blaze
Weaknesses: Water, Ground, Rock

POKÉMON SCARLET:
It lies on warm rocks and uses the heat absorbed by its square-shaped scales to create fire energy.

POKÉMON VIOLET:
Its flame sac is small, so energy is always leaking out. This energy is released from the dent atop Fuecoco's head and flickers to and fro.

Fuecoco → Crocalor → Skeledirge

GABITE

CAVE POKÉMON

How to Say It: gab-BITE
Imperial Height: 4'07"
Metric Height: 1.4 m
Imperial Weight: 123.5 lbs.
Metric Weight: 56.0 kg
Gender: ♂♀
Abilities: Sand Veil
Weaknesses: Fairy, Ice, Dragon

TYPE:
DRAGON-GROUND

POKÉMON SCARLET:

In rare cases, it molts and sheds its scales. Medicine containing its scales as an ingredient will make a weary body feel invigorated.

POKÉMON VIOLET:

It loves sparkly things. It seeks treasures in caves and hoards the loot in its nest.

Gible → **Gabite** → **Garchomp**

GALLADE

BLADE POKÉMON

How to Say It: guh-LADE
Imperial Height: 5'03"
Metric Height: 1.6 m
Imperial Weight: 114.6 lbs.
Metric Weight: 52.0 kg
Gender: ♂
Abilities: Steadfast, Sharpness
Weaknesses: Ghost, Fairy, Flying

TYPE:
PSYCHIC-FIGHTING

POKÉMON SCARLET:

When trying to protect someone, it extends its elbows as if they were swords and fights savagely.

POKÉMON VIOLET:

Because it can sense what its foe is thinking, its attacks burst out first, fast, and fierce.

Ralts → **Kirlia** → **Gallade**

GARCHOMP

MACH POKÉMON

TYPE:
DRAGON-
GROUND

How to Say It: GAR-chomp
Imperial Height: 6'03"
Metric Height: 1.9 m
Imperial Weight: 209.4 lbs.
Metric Weight: 95.0 kg
Gender: ♂♀
Abilities: Sand Veil
Weaknesses: Fairy, Ice, Dragon

POKÉMON SCARLET:

It is said that when one runs at high speed, its wings create blades of wind that can fell nearby trees.

POKÉMON VIOLET:

The protuberances on its head serve as sensors. It can even detect distant prey.

Gible → **Gabite** → **Garchomp**

GARDEVOIR

EMBRACE POKÉMON

How to Say It: GAR-deh-VWAR
Imperial Height: 5'03"
Metric Height: 1.6 m
Imperial Weight: 106.7 lbs.
Metric Weight: 48.4 kg
Gender: ♂♀
Abilities: Synchronize, Trace
Weaknesses: Ghost, Steel, Poison

TYPE:
PSYCHIC-
FAIRY

POKÉMON SCARLET:

To protect its Trainer, it will expend all its psychic power to create a small black hole.

POKÉMON VIOLET:

It unleashes psychokinetic energy at full power when protecting a Trainer it has bonded closely with.

 Ralts **Kirlia** **Gardevoir**

GARGANACL

ROCK SALT POKÉMON

How to Say It: GAHR-gah-NAK-ull
Imperial Height: 7'07"
Metric Height: 2.3 m
Imperial Weight: 529.1 lbs.
Metric Weight: 240.0 kg
Gender: ♂♀
Abilities: Sturdy, Purifying Salt
Weaknesses: Water, Steel, Grass, Fighting, Ground

TYPE: ROCK

POKÉMON SCARLET:

Garganacl will rub its fingertips together and sprinkle injured Pokémon with salt. Even severe wounds will promptly heal afterward.

POKÉMON VIOLET:

Many Pokémon gather around Garganacl, hoping to lick at its mineral-rich salt.

Nacli → Naclstack → Garganacl

TYPE: GHOST-POISON

GASTLY

GAS POKÉMON

How to Say It: GAST-lee
Imperial Height: 4'03"
Metric Height: 1.3 m
Imperial Weight: 0.2 lbs.
Metric Weight: 0.1 kg
Gender: ♂♀
Abilities: Levitate
Weaknesses: Ghost, Dark, Psychic, Ground

POKÉMON SCARLET:

It wraps its opponent in its gas-like body, slowly weakening its prey by poisoning it through the skin.

POKÉMON VIOLET:

Its body is made of gas. Despite lacking substance, it can envelop an opponent of any size and cause suffocation.

Gastly → Haunter → Gengar

GASTRODON

SEA SLUG POKÉMON

WEST SEA

EAST SEA

TYPE:
WATER-GROUND

How to Say It: GAS-stroh-don
Imperial Height: 2'11"
Metric Height: 0.9 m
Imperial Weight: 65.9 lbs.
Metric Weight: 29.9 kg
Gender: ♂♀
Abilities: Sticky Hold, Storm Drain
Weaknesses: Grass

POKÉMON SCARLET:

Its whole body is sticky with mucus. In the past, this form of Gastrodon was by far the more numerous one.

POKÉMON VIOLET:

It appears on beaches where the waters are shallow. Once it catches prey, it will slowly melt them with its mucus before slurping them up.

Shellos → Gastrodon

GENGAR

SHADOW POKÉMON

How to Say It: GHEN-gar
Imperial Height: 4'11"
Metric Height: 1.5 m
Imperial Weight: 89.3 lbs.
Metric Weight: 40.5 kg
Gender: ♂♀
Abilities: Cursed Body
Weaknesses: Ghost, Dark, Psychic, Ground

TYPE:
GHOST-POISON

POKÉMON SCARLET:

To steal the life of its target, it slips into the prey's shadow and silently waits for an opportunity.

POKÉMON VIOLET:

Hiding in people's shadows at night, it absorbs their heat. The chill it causes makes the victims shake.

Gastly → Haunter → Gengar

GHOLDENGO

COIN ENTITY POKÉMON

How to Say It: GOHL-den-goh
Imperial Height: 3'11"
Metric Height: 1.2 m
Imperial Weight: 66.1 lbs.
Metric Weight: 30.0 kg
Gender: Unknown
Abilities: Good as Gold
Weaknesses: Fire, Ghost, Dark, Ground

TYPE: STEEL-GHOST

POKÉMON SCARLET:

Its body seems to be made up of 1,000 coins. This Pokémon gets along well with others and is quick to make friends with anybody.

POKÉMON VIOLET:

It has a sturdy body made up of stacked coins. Gholdengo overwhelms its enemies by firing coin after coin at them in quick succession.

Gimmighoul ⇨ Gholdengo

84

GIBLE

LAND SHARK POKÉMON

TYPE: DRAGON-GROUND

How to Say It: GIB-bull
Imperial Height: 2'04"
Metric Height: 0.7 m
Imperial Weight: 45.2 lbs.
Metric Weight: 20.5 kg
Gender: ♂♀
Abilities: Sand Veil
Weaknesses: Fairy, Ice, Dragon

POKÉMON SCARLET:

It skulks in caves, and when prey or an enemy passes by, it leaps out and chomps them. The force of its attack sometimes chips its teeth.

POKÉMON VIOLET:

It nests in horizontal holes warmed by geothermal heat. Foes who get too close can expect to be pounced on and bitten.

Gible → Gabite → Garchomp

GIMMIGHOUL

COIN CHEST POKÉMON

TYPE: GHOST

How to Say It: GIH-mee-ghoul
Imperial Height: 1'00"
Metric Height: 0.3 m
Imperial Weight: 11.0 lbs.
Metric Weight: 5.0 kg
Gender: Unknown
Abilities: Rattled
Weaknesses: Ghost, Dark

POKÉMON SCARLET:

This Pokémon was born inside a treasure chest about 1,500 years ago. It sucks the life force out of scoundrels who try to steal the treasure.

POKÉMON VIOLET:

It lives inside an old treasure chest. Sometimes it gets left in shop corners since no one realizes it's actually a Pokémon.

Gimmighoul → Gholdengo

GIRAFARIG

LONG NECK POKÉMON

How to Say It: jir-RAF-uh-rig
Imperial Height: 4'11"
Metric Height: 1.5 m
Imperial Weight: 91.5 lbs.
Metric Weight: 41.5 kg
Gender: ♂♀
Abilities: Inner Focus, Early Bird
Weaknesses: Dark, Bug

TYPE:
NORMAL-PSYCHIC

POKÉMON SCARLET:

Though very small, the brain in its tail is still considered an important organ because it emits powerful psychic energy.

POKÉMON VIOLET:

Girafarig's tail has a small head. It instinctively bites at any foe that approaches the Pokémon from behind.

Girafarig   **Farigiraf**

GLACEON

FRESH SNOW POKÉMON

How to Say It: GLAY-cee-on
Imperial Height: 2'07"
Metric Height: 0.8 m
Imperial Weight: 57.1 lbs.
Metric Weight: 25.9 kg
Gender: ♂♀
Abilities: Snow Cloak
Weaknesses: Fire, Steel, Fighting, Rock

TYPE:
ICE

POKÉMON SCARLET:

It can control its body temperature at will. This enables it to freeze the moisture in the atmosphere, creating flurries of diamond dust.

POKÉMON VIOLET:

It lowers its body heat to freeze its fur. The hairs then become like needles it can fire.

Eevee   **Glaceon**

GLALIE

FACE POKÉMON

TYPE:

ICE

How to Say It: GLAY-lee
Imperial Height: 4'11"
Metric Height: 1.5 m
Imperial Weight: 565.5 lbs.
Metric Weight: 265.5 kg
Gender: ♂ ♀
Abilities: Inner Focus, Ice Body
Weaknesses: Fire, Steel, Fighting, Rock

POKÉMON SCARLET:

Its prey is instantaneously frozen stiff by the cold air it exhales from its huge mouth. While they're in that frozen state, it gobbles them up.

POKÉMON VIOLET:

It prevents prey from escaping by instantaneously freezing moisture in the air.

Snorunt   Glalie

GLIMMET

ORE POKÉMON

How to Say It: GLIHM-miht
Imperial Height: 2'04"
Metric Height: 0.7 m
Imperial Weight: 17.6 lbs.
Metric Weight: 8.0 kg
Gender: ♂ ♀
Abilities: Toxic Debris
Weaknesses: Steel, Water, Psychic, Ground

TYPE:

ROCK-POISON

POKÉMON SCARLET:

It absorbs nutrients from cave walls. The petals it wears are made of crystallized poison.

POKÉMON VIOLET:

Glimmet's toxic mineral crystals look just like flower petals. This Pokémon scatters poisonous powder like pollen to protect itself.

Glimmet Glimmora

87

GLIMMORA

ORE POKÉMON

How to Say It: glihm-MOR-uh
Imperial Height: 4'11"
Metric Height: 1.5 m
Imperial Weight: 99.2 lbs.
Metric Weight: 45.0 kg
Gender: ♂♀
Abilities: Toxic Debris
Weaknesses: Steel, Water, Psychic, Ground

TYPE: ROCK-POISON

POKÉMON SCARLET:

When this Pokémon detects danger, it will open up its crystalline petals and fire beams from its conical body.

POKÉMON VIOLET:

Glimmora's petals are made of crystallized poison energy. It has recently become evident that these petals resemble Tera Jewels.

Glimmet → Glimmora

GOGOAT

MOUNT POKÉMON

How to Say It: GO-goat
Imperial Height: 5'07"
Metric Height: 1.7 m
Imperial Weight: 200.6 lbs.
Metric Weight: 91.0 kg
Gender: ♂♀
Abilities: Sap Sipper
Weaknesses: Fire, Flying, Ice, Poison, Bug

TYPE: GRASS

POKÉMON SCARLET:

It can sense the feelings of others by touching them with its horns. This species has assisted people with their work since 5,000 years ago.

POKÉMON VIOLET:

These Pokémon live in herds in mountainous places. The victor in their contests of clashing horns will become the leader of the herd.

Skiddo → Gogoat

GOLDUCK

DUCK POKÉMON

TYPE:
WATER

How to Say It: GOL-duck
Imperial Height: 5'07"
Metric Height: 1.7 m
Imperial Weight: 168.9 lbs.
Metric Weight: 76.6 kg
Gender: ♂♀
Abilities: Damp, Cloud Nine
Weaknesses: Grass, Electric

POKÉMON SCARLET:

When it swims at full speed using its long, webbed limbs, its forehead somehow begins to glow.

POKÉMON VIOLET:

It swims gracefully along on the quiet, slow-moving rivers and lakes of which it is so fond.

Psyduck   Golduck

GOODRA

DRAGON POKÉMON

TYPE:
DRAGON

How to Say It: GOO-druh
Imperial Height: 6'07"
Metric Height: 2.0 m
Imperial Weight: 331.8 lbs.
Metric Weight: 150.5 kg
Gender: ♂♀
Abilities: Hydration, Sap Sipper
Weaknesses: Fairy, Ice, Dragon

POKÉMON SCARLET:

It loves the rain. This mellow Pokémon can be seen walking around on the plains and in the mountains on rainy days.

POKÉMON VIOLET:

This Pokémon is uncontrollable when enraged. It rampages on and on, lashing its tail with enough power to send a dump truck flying.

Goomy   Sliggoo   Goodra

GOOMY

SOFT TISSUE POKÉMON

How to Say It: GOO-mee
Imperial Height: 1'00"
Metric Height: 0.3 m
Imperial Weight: 6.2 lbs.
Metric Weight: 2.8 kg
Gender: ♂♀
Abilities: Hydration, Sap Sipper
Weaknesses: Fairy, Ice, Dragon

TYPE:
DRAGON

POKÉMON SCARLET:

Most of a Goomy's body is water. A membrane covers the whole Pokémon to prevent it from shriveling up in dry weather.

POKÉMON VIOLET:

Goomy's horns are excellent sensory organs that cover all five of Goomy's senses. Goomy picks up on danger from the movement of the air.

Goomy → Sliggoo → Goodra

GOTHITA

FIXATION POKÉMON

TYPE:
PSYCHIC

How to Say It: GAH-THEE-tah
Imperial Height: 1'04"
Metric Height: 0.4 m
Imperial Weight: 12.8 lbs.
Metric Weight: 5.8 kg
Gender: ♂♀
Abilities: Frisk, Competitive
Weaknesses: Ghost, Dark, Bug

POKÉMON SCARLET:

This Pokémon is normally very innocent. When it is staring at something invisible, it is unblinking and utterly silent.

POKÉMON VIOLET:

Beware of touching the ribbon-shaped feelers that control its psychic power. Gothita will begin bawling if you do.

Gothita → Gothorita → Gothitelle

GOTHITELLE

ASTRAL BODY POKÉMON

How to Say It: GAH-thih-tell
Imperial Height: 4'11"
Metric Height: 1.5 m
Imperial Weight: 97.0 lbs.
Metric Weight: 44.0 kg
Gender: ♂♀
Abilities: Frisk, Competitive
Weaknesses: Ghost, Dark, Bug

TYPE:
PSYCHIC

POKÉMON SCARLET:

Gothitelle unleashes psychic energy and shows opponents dreams of the universe's end. These dreams are apparently ethereal and beautiful.

POKÉMON VIOLET:

It gazes at the stars to predict the future. It acts somewhat detached because it has seen the end of all existence.

Gothita → Gothorita → Gothitelle

GOTHORITA

MANIPULATE POKÉMON

How to Say It: GAH-thoh-REE-tah
Imperial Height: 2'04"
Metric Height: 0.7 m
Imperial Weight: 39.7 lbs.
Metric Weight: 18.0 kg
Gender: ♂♀
Abilities: Frisk, Competitive
Weaknesses: Ghost, Dark, Bug

TYPE:
PSYCHIC

POKÉMON SCARLET:

This Pokémon will hypnotize children to put them to sleep before carrying them away. Be wary of nights when the starlight is bright.

POKÉMON VIOLET:

Using its psychic power, it arranges pebbles to form the shapes of constellations. Some people believe this Pokémon came from outer space.

Gothita Gothorita Gothitelle

GRAFAIAI

TOXIC MONKEY POKÉMON

How to Say It: gruh-FEYE-eye
Imperial Height: 2'04"
Metric Height: 0.7 m
Imperial Weight: 60.0 lbs.
Metric Weight: 27.2 kg
Gender: ♂♀
Abilities: Unburden, Poison Touch
Weaknesses: Psychic, Ground

TYPE: POISON-NORMAL

POKÉMON SCARLET:

The color of the poisonous saliva depends on what the Pokémon eats. Grafaiai covers its fingers in its saliva and draws patterns on trees in forests.

POKÉMON VIOLET:

Each Grafaiai paints its own individual pattern, and it will paint that same pattern over and over again throughout its life.

Shroodle   **Grafaiai**

GREAT TUSK

PARADOX POKÉMON

TYPE: GROUND-FIGHTING

How to Say It: GREAT TUSK
Imperial Height: 7'03"
Metric Height: 2.2 m
Imperial Weight: 705.5 lbs.
Metric Weight: 320.0 kg
Gender: Unknown
Abilities: Protosynthesis
Weaknesses: Psychic, Flying, Ice, Water, Fairy, Grass

POKÉMON SCARLET:

Sightings of this Pokémon have occurred in recent years. The name Great Tusk was taken from a creature listed in a certain book.

POKÉMON VIOLET:

This creature resembles a mysterious Pokémon that, according to a paranormal magazine, has lived since ancient times.

Does not evolve.

GREAVARD

GHOST DOG POKÉMON

TYPE:

GHOST

How to Say It: GREE-verd
Imperial Height: 2'00"
Metric Height: 0.6 m
Imperial Weight: 77.2 lbs.
Metric Weight: 35.0 kg
Gender: ♂♀
Abilities: Pickup
Weaknesses: Ghost, Dark

POKÉMON SCARLET:

It is said that a dog Pokémon that died in the wild without ever interacting with a human was reborn as this Pokémon.

POKÉMON VIOLET:

This friendly Pokémon doesn't like being alone. Pay it even the slightest bit of attention, and it will follow you forever.

Greavard → Houndstone

GREEDENT

GREEDY POKÉMON

How to Say It: GREE-dent
Imperial Height: 2'00"
Metric Height: 0.6 m
Imperial Weight: 13.2 lbs.
Metric Weight: 6.0 kg
Gender: ♂♀
Abilities: Cheek Pouch
Weaknesses: Fighting

TYPE:

NORMAL

POKÉMON SCARLET:

If it spots a berry tree, it will immediately go to gather berries without a sideways glance—even if it's in the middle of a battle.

POKÉMON VIOLET:

This Pokémon makes off with heaps of fallen berries by wrapping them in its tail, which is roughly twice the length of its body.

Skwovet → Greedent

GRIMER

SLUDGE POKÉMON

How to Say It: GRY-mur
Imperial Height: 2'11"
Metric Height: 0.9 m
Imperial Weight: 66.1 lbs.
Metric Weight: 30.0 kg
Gender: ♂♀
Abilities: Stench, Sticky Hold
Weaknesses: Pyschic, Ground

TYPE:
POISON

POKÉMON SCARLET:
Born from sludge, these Pokémon now gather in polluted places and increase the bacteria in their bodies.

POKÉMON VIOLET:
When two of these Pokémon's bodies are combined together, new poisons are created.

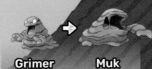

Grimer → Muk

GRIMMSNARL

BULK UP POKÉMON

How to Say It: GRIM-snarl
Imperial Height: 4'11"
Metric Height: 1.5 m
Imperial Weight: 134.5 lbs.
Metric Weight: 61.0 kg
Gender: ♂
Abilities: Frisk, Prankster
Weaknesses: Steel, Fairy, Poison

TYPE:
DARK-FAIRY

POKÉMON SCARLET:
This Pokémon has complete control over its hair. Grimmsnarl normally keeps its hair wrapped around its body to support its muscles.

POKÉMON VIOLET:
It lives deep within the forest. Even after evolving into this splendid form, it hasn't given up on its petty misdeeds and pranks.

Impidimp → Morgrem → Grimmsnarl

GROWLITHE

PUPPY POKÉMON

TYPE: FIRE

How to Say It: GROWL-lith
Imperial Height: 2'04"
Metric Height: 0.7 m
Imperial Weight: 41.9 lbs
Metric Weight: 19.0 kg
Gender: ♂♀
Abilities: Intimidate, Flash Fire
Weaknesses: Water, Ground, Rock

POKÉMON SCARLET:
It has a brave and trustworthy nature. It fearlessly stands up to bigger and stronger foes.

POKÉMON VIOLET:
It's very friendly and faithful to people. It will try to repel enemies by barking and biting.

Growlithe → Arcanine

GRUMPIG

MANIPULATE POKÉMON

How to Say It: GRUM-pig
Imperial Height: 2'11"
Metric Height: 0.9 m
Imperial Weight: 157.6 lbs.
Metric Weight: 71.5 kg
Gender: ♂♀
Abilities: Thick Fat, Own Tempo
Weaknesses: Ghost, Dark, Bug

TYPE: PSYCHIC

POKÉMON SCARLET:
It can perform odd dance steps to influence foes. Its style of dancing became hugely popular overseas.

POKÉMON VIOLET:
It uses black pearls to amplify its psychic power. It does a strange dance to control foes' minds.

Spoink → Grumpig

GULPIN

STOMACH POKÉMON

How to Say It: GULL-pin
Imperial Height: 1'04"
Metric Height: 0.4 m
Imperial Weight: 22.7 lbs.
Metric Weight: 10.3 kg
Gender: ♂♀
Abilities: Liquid Ooze, Sticky Hold
Weaknesses: Psychic, Ground

TYPE:
POISON

POKÉMON SCARLET:
There is nothing its stomach can't digest. While it is digesting, vile, overpowering gases are expelled.

POKÉMON VIOLET:
It has a small heart and brain. Its stomach comprises most of its body, with enzymes to dissolve anything.

Gulpin → **Swalot**

GUMSHOOS

STAKEOUT POKÉMON

How to Say It: GUM-shooss
Imperial Height: 2'04"
Metric Height: 0.7 m
Imperial Weight: 31.3 lbs.
Metric Weight: 14.2 kg
Gender: ♂♀
Abilities: Strong Jaw, Stakeout
Weaknesses: Fighting

TYPE:
NORMAL

POKÉMON SCARLET:
Once it finds signs of prey, it will patiently stake out the location, waiting until the sun goes down.

POKÉMON VIOLET:
Gumshoos specializes in relentlessly tracking down prey. The simple-minded Skwovet doesn't seem to provide Gumshoos enough challenge.

Yungoos Gumshoos

GYARADOS

ATROCIOUS POKÉMON

TYPE:
WATER-FLYING

How to Say It: GARE-uh-dos
Imperial Height: 21'04"
Metric Height: 6.5 m
Imperial Weight: 518.1 lbs.
Metric Weight: 235.0 kg
Gender: ♂♀
Abilities: Intimidate
Weaknesses: Electric, Rock

POKÉMON SCARLET:

Once it appears, it goes on a rampage. It remains enraged until it demolishes everything around it.

POKÉMON VIOLET:

It appears whenever there is world conflict, burning down any place it travels through.

Magikarp   **Gyarados**

HAPPINY

PLAYHOUSE POKÉMON

How to Say It: hap-PEE-nee
Imperial Height: 2'00"
Metric Height: 0.6 m
Imperial Weight: 53.8 lbs.
Metric Weight: 24.4 kg
Gender: ♀
Abilities: Natural Cure, Serene Grace
Weaknesses: Fighting

TYPE:
NORMAL

POKÉMON SCARLET:

It carries a round, white rock in its belly pouch. If it gets along well with someone, it will sometimes give that person the rock.

POKÉMON VIOLET:

It carefully carries a round, white rock that it thinks is an egg. It's bothered by how curly its hair looks.

 Happiny   **Chansey**   **Blissey**

HARIYAMA

ARM THRUST POKÉMON

How to Say It: HAR-ee-YAH-mah
Imperial Height: 7'07"
Metric Height: 2.3 m
Imperial Weight: 559.5 lbs.
Metric Weight: 253.8 kg
Gender: ♂♀
Abilities: Guts, Thick Fat
Weaknesses: Psychic, Flying, Fairy

TYPE: FIGHTING

POKÉMON SCARLET:

It loves challenging others to tests of strength. It has the power to stop a train with a slap.

POKÉMON VIOLET:

It stomps on the ground to build power. It can send a 10-ton truck flying with a straight-arm punch.

Makuhita → Hariyama

HATENNA

CALM POKÉMON

TYPE: PSYCHIC

How to Say It: hat-EN-nuh
Imperial Height: 1'04"
Metric Height: 0.4 m
Imperial Weight: 7.5 lbs.
Metric Weight: 3.4 kg
Gender: ♀
Abilities: Anticipation, Healer
Weaknesses: Ghost, Dark, Bug

POKÉMON SCARLET:

Because the emotions of others constantly flow into its head, this Pokémon prefers environments where no other creatures live.

POKÉMON VIOLET:

It senses the feelings of other living creatures. Be careful not to expose it to strong emotions for too long, or it will end up exhausted.

Hatenna → Hattrem → Hatterene

HATTERENE

SILENT POKÉMON

TYPE: PSYCHIC-FAIRY

How to Say It: HAT-eh-reen
Imperial Height: 6'11"
Metric Height: 2.1 m
Imperial Weight: 11.2 lbs.
Metric Weight: 5.1 kg
Gender: ♀
Abilities: Anticipation, Healer
Weaknesses: Ghost, Steel, Poison

POKÉMON SCARLET:
Hatterene knocks out those that intrude in its home forest by blasting them with a beam, then slashing with claws enhanced by psychic power.

POKÉMON VIOLET:
Beware of forests that show no signs of living creatures within. You may have wandered into Hatterene's territory.

Hatenna → Hattrem → Hatterene

HATTREM

SERENE POKÉMON

TYPE: PSYCHIC

How to Say It: HAT-trum
Imperial Height: 2'00"
Metric Height: 0.6 m
Imperial Weight: 10.6 lbs.
Metric Weight: 4.8 kg
Gender: ♀
Abilities: Anticipation, Healer
Weaknesses: Ghost, Dark, Bug

POKÉMON SCARLET:
To this Pokémon, strong emotions apparently feel like incredibly loud noises—even if the emotions are happy ones.

POKÉMON VIOLET:
The moment this Pokémon finds someone who's emitting strong emotions, it will pummel them senseless with its braids to silence them.

Hatenna → Hattrem → Hatterene

HAUNTER

GAS POKÉMON

How to Say It: HAUNT-ur
Imperial Height: 5'03"
Metric Height: 1.6 m
Imperial Weight: 0.2 lbs.
Metric Weight: 0.1 kg
Gender: ♂♀
Abilities: Levitate
Weaknesses: Ghost, Dark, Psychic, Ground

**TYPE:
GHOST-POISON**

POKÉMON SCARLET:

It likes to lurk in the dark and tap shoulders with a gaseous hand. Its touch causes endless shuddering.

POKÉMON VIOLET:

In total darkness, where nothing is visible, Haunter lurks, silently stalking its next victim.

Gastly   Haunter   Gengar

HAWLUCHA

WRESTLING POKÉMON

**TYPE:
FIGHTING-FLYING**

How to Say It: haw-LOO-cha
Imperial Height: 2'07"
Metric Height: 0.8 m
Imperial Weight: 47.4 lbs.
Metric Weight: 21.5 kg
Gender: ♂♀
Abilities: Limber, Unburden
Weaknesses: Psychic, Flying, Fairy, Electric, Ice

POKÉMON SCARLET:

Its elegant finishing moves—performed by nimbly leaping around using its wings—are polished in the forest where it was born and raised.

POKÉMON VIOLET:

Hawlucha live quietly without flocking together. They fight constantly with their natural enemies: noisy groups of Primeape.

Does not evolve.

HAXORUS

AXE JAW POKÉMON

TYPE: DRAGON

How to Say It: HAK-soar-us
Imperial Height: 5'11"
Metric Height: 1.8 m
Imperial Weight: 232.6 lbs.
Metric Weight: 105.5 kg
Gender: ♂ ♀
Abilities: Rivalry, Mold Breaker
Weaknesses: Fairy, Ice, Dragon

POKÉMON SCARLET:

This Pokémon nests in caves and abandoned mines. It is docile, but it will become incredibly angry if its tusks are touched, so beware.

POKÉMON VIOLET:

It overwhelms enemies with its prized tusks, which are sharp enough to cut through a metal transmission tower in one strike.

Axew ➡ Fraxure ➡ Haxorus

HERACROSS

SINGLE HORN POKÉMON

How to Say It: HAIR-uh-cross
Imperial Height: 4'11"
Metric Height: 1.5 m
Imperial Weight: 119.0 lbs.
Metric Weight: 54.0 kg
Gender: ♂ ♀
Abilities: Swarm, Guts
Weaknesses: Fire, Psychic, Flying, Fairy

TYPE: BUG-FIGHTING

POKÉMON SCARLET:

It loves sweet nectar. To keep all the nectar to itself, it hurls rivals away with its prized horn.

POKÉMON VIOLET:

With its herculean powers, it can easily throw around an object that is 100 times its own weight.

Does not evolve.

HIPPOPOTAS

HIPPO POKÉMON

How to Say It: HIP-poh-puh-TOSS
Imperial Height: 2'07"
Metric Height: 0.8 m
Imperial Weight: 109.1 lbs.
Metric Weight: 49.5 kg
Gender: ♂ ♀
Abilities: Sand Stream
Weaknesses: Water, Grass, Ice

TYPE: GROUND

POKÉMON SCARLET:

It shuts its nostrils tight, then travels through sand as if walking. They form colonies of around 10.

POKÉMON VIOLET:

It shrouds itself in sand to ward off germs. It travels easily through the sands of the desert.

Hippopotas → Hippowdon

HIPPOWDON

HEAVYWEIGHT POKÉMON

TYPE: GROUND

How to Say It: hip-POW-don
Imperial Height: 6'07"
Metric Height: 2.0 m
Imperial Weight: 661.4 lbs.
Metric Weight: 300.0 kg
Gender: ♂ ♀
Abilities: Sand Stream
Weaknesses: Water, Grass, Ice

POKÉMON SCARLET:

It is surprisingly quick to anger. It holds its mouth agape as a display of its strength.

POKÉMON VIOLET:

It brandishes its gaping mouth in a display of fearsome strength. It raises vast quantities of sand while attacking.

Hippopotas → Hippowdon

HONCHKROW

TYPE:
DARK-FLYING

How to Say It: HONCH-krow
Imperial Height: 2'11"
Metric Height: 0.9 m
Imperial Weight: 60.2 lbs.
Metric Weight: 27.3 kg
Gender: ♂ ♀
Abilities: Insomnia, Super Luck
Weaknesses: Fairy, Electric, Ice, Rock

POKÉMON SCARLET:
It is merciless by nature. It is said that it never forgives the mistakes of its Murkrow followers.

POKÉMON VIOLET:
A single cry from this nocturnal Pokémon, and more than 100 of its Murkrow cronies will assemble.

Murkrow → Honchkrow

HOPPIP

COTTONWEED POKÉMON

How to Say It: HOP-pip
Imperial Height: 1'04"
Metric Height: 0.4 m
Imperial Weight: 1.1 lbs.
Metric Weight: 0.5 kg
Gender: ♂ ♀
Abilities: Chlorophyll, Leaf Guard
Weaknesses: Fire, Flying, Ice, Poison, Rock

TYPE:
GRASS-FLYING

POKÉMON SCARLET:
This Pokémon is blown across vast distances by the wind. It is unclear where the Hoppip of Paldea originally came from.

POKÉMON VIOLET:
Outside of cold regions, Hoppip can be found practically everywhere. This is because the wind carries this species all over the world.

Hoppip → Skiploom → Jumpluff

HOUNDOOM

DARK POKÉMON

How to Say It: HOWN-doom
Imperial Height: 4'07"
Metric Height: 1.4 m
Imperial Weight: 77.2 lbs.
Metric Weight: 35.0 kg
Gender: ♂♀
Abilities: Flash Fire, Early Bird
Weaknesses: Water, Ground, Fighting, Rock

TYPE: DARK-FIRE

POKÉMON SCARLET:
If you are burned by the flames it shoots from its mouth, the pain will never go away.

POKÉMON VIOLET:
Upon hearing its eerie howls, other Pokémon get the shivers and head straight back to their nests.

Houndour → Houndoom

HOUNDOUR

DARK POKÉMON

How to Say It: HOWN-dowr
Imperial Height: 2'00"
Metric Height: 0.6 m
Imperial Weight: 23.8 lbs.
Metric Weight: 10.8 kg
Gender: ♂♀
Abilities: Flash Fire, Early Bird
Weaknesses: Water, Ground, Fighting, Rock

TYPE: DARK-FIRE

POKÉMON SCARLET:
It is smart enough to hunt in packs. It uses a variety of cries for communicating with others.

POKÉMON VIOLET:
It uses different kinds of cries for communicating with others of its kind and for pursuing its prey.

Houndour → Houndoom

HOUNDSTONE

GHOST DOG POKÉMON

TYPE:

GHOST

How to Say It: HOUND-stone
Imperial Height: 6'07"
Metric Height: 2.0 m
Imperial Weight: 33.1 lbs.
Metric Weight: 15.0 kg
Gender: ♂ ♀
Abilities: Sand Rush
Weaknesses: Ghost, Dark

POKÉMON SCARLET:

Houndstone spends most of its time sleeping in graveyards. Among all the dog Pokémon, this one is most loyal to its master.

POKÉMON VIOLET:

A lovingly mourned Pokémon was reborn as Houndstone. It doesn't like anyone touching the protuberance atop its head.

Greavard   Houndstone

HYDREIGON

BRUTAL POKÉMON

How to Say It: hy-DRY-guhn
Imperial Height: 5'11"
Metric Height: 1.8 m
Imperial Weight: 352.7 lbs.
Metric Weight: 160.0 kg
Gender: ♂♀
Abilities: Levitate
Weaknesses: Fairy, Fighting, Bug, Ice, Dragon

TYPE: DARK-DRAGON

POKÉMON SCARLET:

Only the central head has a brain. It is very intelligent, but it thinks only of destruction.

POKÉMON VIOLET:

It's said that Hydreigon grew ferocious because people in times long past loathed it, considering it to be evil incarnate and attacking it relentlessly.

Deino → Zweilous → Hydreigon

HYPNO

HYPNOSIS POKÉMON

TYPE: PSYCHIC

How to Say It: HIP-no
Imperial Height: 5'03"
Metric Height: 1.6 m
Imperial Weight: 166.7 lbs.
Metric Weight: 75.6 kg
Gender: ♂♀
Abilities: Insomnia, Forewarn
Weaknesses: Ghost, Dark, Bug

POKÉMON SCARLET:

When it locks eyes with an enemy, it will use a mix of psi moves, such as Hypnosis and Confusion.

POKÉMON VIOLET:

Always holding a pendulum that it swings at a steady rhythm, it causes drowsiness in anyone nearby.

Drowzee → Hypno

IGGLYBUFF

BALLOON POKÉMON

TYPE:
NORMAL-
FAIRY

How to Say It: IG-lee-buff
Imperial Height: 1'00"
Metric Height: 0.3 m
Imperial Weight: 2.2 lbs.
Metric Weight: 1.0 kg
Gender: ♂♀
Abilities: Cute Charm, Competitive
Weaknesses: Steel, Poison

POKÉMON SCARLET:
Its body has a faintly sweet scent and is bouncy and soft. If it bounces even once, it cannot stop.

POKÉMON VIOLET:
It likes to sing but is not yet good at it. With praise and encouragement, it will get better little by little.

Igglybuff → Jigglypuff → Wigglytuff

IMPIDIMP

WILY POKÉMON

How to Say It: IMP-ih-dimp
Imperial Height: 1'04"
Metric Height: 0.4 m
Imperial Weight: 12.1 lbs.
Metric Weight: 5.5 kg
Gender: ♂
Abilities: Frisk, Prankster
Weaknesses: Steel, Fairy, Poison

TYPE:
DARK-
FAIRY

POKÉMON SCARLET:
The reason this Pokémon causes trouble for those it feels close to is because Impidimp itself gets irritable if it can't absorb negative emotions.

POKÉMON VIOLET:
They live in groups, pestering and playing pranks on each other to polish their troublemaking skills.

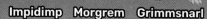

Impidimp → Morgrem → Grimmsnarl

INDEEDEE

EMOTION POKÉMON

How to Say It: in-DEE-dee
Imperial Height: 2'11"
Metric Height: 0.9 m
Imperial Weight: 61.7 lbs.
Metric Weight: 28.0 kg
Gender: ♂♀
Abilities: Synchronize, Inner Focus (Male), Own Tempo (Female)
Weaknesses: Dark, Bug

MALE

MALE

POKÉMON SCARLET:

This Pokémon picks up on the positive emotions of other creatures via its horns and uses those emotions to fuel itself.

POKÉMON VIOLET:

This Pokémon never leaves its Trainer's side. It predicts their actions with its psychic power and takes care of their day-to-day needs.

TYPE:

PSYCHIC-NORMAL

FEMALE

FEMALE

POKÉMON SCARLET:

It dislikes conflict. If a fight occurs in its territory, it uses psychic power to throw things at the combatants in an effort to drive them away.

POKÉMON VIOLET:

In search of happy feelings—such as joy and gratitude—Indeedee bustles around, taking diligent care of people and other Pokémon.

Does not evolve.

IRON BUNDLE

PARADOX POKÉMON

TYPE:
ICE-WATER

How to Say It: EYE-ern BUN-del
Imperial Height: 2'00"
Metric Height: 0.6 m
Imperial Weight: 24.3 lbs.
Metric Weight: 11.0 kg
Gender: Unknown
Abilities: Quark Drive
Weaknesses: Grass, Electric, Fighting, Rock

POKÉMON SCARLET:

Its shape is similar to a robot featured in a paranormal magazine article. The robot was said to have been created by an ancient civilization.

POKÉMON VIOLET:

It resembles a mysterious object mentioned in an old book. There are only two reported sightings of this Pokémon.

Does not evolve.

IRON HANDS

PARADOX POKÉMON

TYPE:
FIGHTING-ELECTRIC

How to Say It: EYE-ern HANDS
Imperial Height: 5'11"
Metric Height: 1.8 m
Imperial Weight: 893.3 lbs.
Metric Weight: 380.7 kg
Gender: Unknown
Abilities: Quark Drive
Weaknesses: Psychic, Fairy, Ground

POKÉMON SCARLET:

It is very similar to a cyborg covered exclusively by a paranormal magazine. The cyborg was said to be the modified form of a certain athlete.

POKÉMON VIOLET:

This Pokémon shares many similarities with Iron Hands, an object mentioned in a certain expedition journal.

Does not evolve.

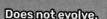

IRON JUGULIS

PARADOX POKÉMON

How to Say It: EYE-ern JUH-gyoo-lihs
Imperial Height: 4'03"
Metric Height: 1.3 m
Imperial Weight: 244.7 lbs.
Metric Weight: 111.0 kg
Gender: Unknown
Abilities: Quark Drive
Weaknesses: Fairy, Electric, Ice, Rock

**TYPE:
DARK-
FLYING**

POKÉMON SCARLET:

It resembles a certain Pokémon introduced in a paranormal magazine, described as the offspring of a Hydreigon that fell in love with a robot.

POKÉMON VIOLET:

It's possible that Iron Jugulis, an object described in an old book, may actually be this Pokémon.

Does not evolve.

IRON MOTH

PARADOX POKÉMON

**TYPE:
FIRE-
POISON**

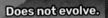

How to Say It: EYE-ern MAHTH
Imperial Height: 3'11"
Metric Height: 1.2 m
Imperial Weight: 79.4 lbs.
Metric Weight: 36.0 kg
Gender: Unknown
Abilities: Quark Drive
Weaknesses: Water, Psychic, Ground, Rock

POKÉMON SCARLET:

This Pokémon resembles an unknown object described in a paranormal magazine as a UFO sent to observe humanity.

POKÉMON VIOLET:

No records exist of this species being caught. Data is lacking, but the Pokémon's traits match up with an object described in an old book.

Does not evolve.

IRON THORNS

PARADOX POKÉMON

**TYPE:
ROCK-
ELECTRIC**

How to Say It: EYE-ern THORNS
Imperial Height: 5'03"
Metric Height: 1.6 m
Imperial Weight: 668.0 lbs.
Metric Weight: 303.0 kg
Gender: Unknown
Abilities: Quark Drive
Weaknesses: Water, Grass, Fighting, Ground

POKÉMON SCARLET:

It has some similarities to a Pokémon introduced in a dubious magazine as a Tyranitar from one billion years into the future.

POKÉMON VIOLET:

Some of its notable features match those of an object named within a certain expedition journal as Iron Thorns.

Does not evolve.

IRON TREADS

PARADOX POKÉMON

How to Say It: EYE-ern TREDS
Imperial Height: 2'11"
Metric Height: 0.9 m
Imperial Weight: 529.1 lbs.
Metric Weight: 240.0 kg
Gender: Unknown
Abilities: Quark Drive
Weaknesses: Fire, Water, Fighting, Ground

**TYPE:
GROUND-
STEEL**

POKÉMON SCARLET:

This Pokémon closely resembles a scientific weapon that a paranormal magazine claimed was sent to this planet by aliens.

POKÉMON VIOLET:

Sightings of this Pokémon have occurred in recent years. It resembles a mysterious object described in an old expedition journal.

Does not evolve.

IRON VALIANT

PARADOX POKÉMON

How to Say It: EYE-ern VAL-ee-ent
Imperial Height: 4'07"
Metric Height: 1.4 m
Imperial Weight: 77.2 lbs.
Metric Weight: 35.0 kg
Gender: Unknown
Abilities: Quark Drive
Weaknesses: Steel, Psychic, Flying, Fairy, Poison

TYPE: FAIRY-FIGHTING

POKÉMON SCARLET:
It has some similarities to a mad scientist's invention covered in a paranormal magazine.

POKÉMON VIOLET:
It's possible that this is the object listed as Iron Valiant in a certain expedition journal.

Does not evolve.

JIGGLYPUFF

BALLOON POKÉMON

TYPE: NORMAL-FAIRY

How to Say It: JIG-lee-puff
Imperial Height: 1'08"
Metric Height: 0.5 m
Imperial Weight: 12.1 lbs.
Metric Weight: 5.5 kg
Gender: ♂ ♀
Abilities: Cute Charm, Competitive
Weaknesses: Steel, Poison

POKÉMON SCARLET:
When its huge eyes waver, it sings a mysteriously soothing melody that lulls its enemies to sleep.

POKÉMON VIOLET:
If it inflates to sing a lullaby, it can perform longer and cause sure drowsiness in its audience.

Igglybuff → Jigglypuff → Wigglytuff

JOLTEON

LIGHTNING POKÉMON

TYPE: ELECTRIC

How to Say It: JOL-tee-on
Imperial Height: 2'07"
Metric Height: 0.8 m
Imperial Weight: 54.0 lbs.
Metric Weight: 24.5 kg
Gender: ♂♀
Abilities: Volt Absorb
Weaknesses: Ground

POKÉMON SCARLET:
It concentrates the weak electric charges emitted by its cells and launches wicked lightning bolts.

POKÉMON VIOLET:
If agitated, it uses electricity to straighten out its fur and launch it in small bunches.

Eevee → Jolteon

JUMPLUFF

COTTONWEED POKÉMON

How to Say It: JUM-pluff
Imperial Height: 2'07"
Metric Height: 0.8 m
Imperial Weight: 6.6 lbs.
Metric Weight: 3.0 kg
Gender: ♂♀
Abilities: Chlorophyll, Leaf Guard
Weaknesses: Fire, Flying, Ice, Poison, Rock

TYPE: GRASS-FLYING

POKÉMON SCARLET:
Jumpluff travels on seasonal winds. Once its cotton spores run out, its journey ends, as does its life.

POKÉMON VIOLET:
Beware its cotton spores. If you accidentally breathe them in, you'll be racked with coughs and itchiness.

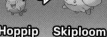

Hoppip → Skiploom → Jumpluff

KILOWATTREL

FRIGATEBIRD POKÉMON

How to Say It: KIH-loh-WAHT-rel
Imperial Height: 4'07"
Metric Height: 1.4 m
Imperial Weight: 85.1 lbs.
Metric Weight: 38.6 kg
Gender: ♂♀
Abilities: Volt Absorb, Wind Power
Weaknesses: Ice, Rock

TYPE: ELECTRIC-FLYING

POKÉMON SCARLET:

Kilowattrel inflates its throat sac to amplify its electricity. By riding the wind, this Pokémon can fly over 430 miles in a day.

POKÉMON VIOLET:

It uses its throat sac to store electricity generated by its wings. There's hardly any oil in its feathers, so it is a poor swimmer.

Wattrel   Kilowattrel

KINGAMBIT

BIG BLADE POKÉMON

How to Say It: kihn-GAM-bet
Imperial Height: 6'07"
Metric Height: 2.0 m
Imperial Weight: 264.6 lbs.
Metric Weight: 120.0 kg
Gender: ♂♀
Abilities: Defiant, Supreme Overlord
Weaknesses: Fire, Fighting, Ground

TYPE: DARK-STEEL

POKÉMON SCARLET:

Only a Bisharp that stands above all others in its vast army can evolve into Kingambit.

POKÉMON VIOLET:

Though it commands a massive army in battle, it's not skilled at devising complex strategies. It just uses brute strength to keep pushing.

Pawniard   Bisharp   Kingambit

KIRLIA

EMOTION POKÉMON

TYPE:
PSYCHIC-FAIRY

How to Say It: KERL-lee-ah
Imperial Height: 2'07"
Metric Height: 0.8 m
Imperial Weight: 44.5 lbs.
Metric Weight: 20.2 kg
Gender: ♂♀
Abilities: Synchronize, Trace
Weaknesses: Ghost, Steel, Poison

POKÉMON SCARLET:

It has a psychic power that enables it to distort the space around it and see into the future.

POKÉMON VIOLET:

The cheerful spirit of its Trainer gives it energy for its psychokinetic power. It spins and dances when happy.

Gardevoir

Ralts → Kirlia

Gallade

KLAWF

AMBUSH POKÉMON

TYPE:
ROCK

How to Say It: KLAWF
Imperial Height: 4'03"
Metric Height: 1.3 m
Imperial Weight: 174.2 lbs.
Metric Weight: 79.0 kg
Gender: ♂♀
Abilities: Shell Armor, Anger Shell
Weaknesses: Water, Steel, Grass, Fighting, Ground

POKÉMON SCARLET:

Klawf hangs upside down from cliffs, waiting for prey. But Klawf can't remain in this position for long because its blood rushes to its head.

POKÉMON VIOLET:

This Pokémon lives on sheer cliffs. It sidesteps opponents' attacks, then lunges for their weak spots with its claws.

Does not evolve.

KLEFKI

KEY RING POKÉMON

How to Say It: KLEF-key
Imperial Height: 0'08"
Metric Height: 0.2 m
Imperial Weight: 6.6 lbs.
Metric Weight: 3.0 kg
Gender: ♂♀
Abilities: Prankster
Weaknesses: Fire, Ground

TYPE:
STEEL-FAIRY

POKÉMON SCARLET:

Once it absorbs a key's metal ions, it discards the key without a second thought. However, it will hang on to keys it favors for decades.

POKÉMON VIOLET:

In the past, noble families entrusted their vault keys to a Klefki. They passed the Klefki down through the generations, taking good care of it.

Does not evolve.

KOMALA

DROWSING POKÉMON

How to Say It: koh-MAH-luh
Imperial Height: 1'04"
Metric Height: 0.4 m
Imperial Weight: 43.9 lbs.
Metric Weight: 19.9 kg
Gender: ♂♀
Abilities: Comatose
Weaknesses: Fighting

TYPE:
NORMAL

POKÉMON SCARLET:

Komala spends its entire life sleeping. It feeds on leaves that contain a potent poison only Komala can break down.

POKÉMON VIOLET:

A potent anesthetic can be made by diluting Komala's drool. This anesthetic was used for surgeries in the past.

Does not evolve.

KORAIDON

PARADOX POKÉMON

POKÉMON SCARLET:

This seems to be the Winged King mentioned in an old expedition journal. It was said to have split the land with its bare fists.

POKÉMON VIOLET:

This Pokémon resembles Cyclizar, but it is far burlier and more ferocious. Nothing is known about its ecology or other features.

TYPE:
FIGHTING-DRAGON

How to Say It: koh-RAI-dahn
Imperial Height: 8'02"
Metric Height: 2.5 m
Imperial Weight: 668.0 lbs.
Metric Weight: 303.0 kg
Gender: Unknown
Abilities: Orichalcum Pulse
Weaknesses: Psychic, Flying, Fairy, Ice, Dragon

Does not evolve.

KRICKETOT

CRICKET POKÉMON

How to Say It: KRICK-eh-tot
Imperial Height: 1'00"
Metric Height: 0.3 m
Imperial Weight: 4.9 lbs.
Metric Weight: 2.2 kg
Gender: ♂♀
Abilities: Shed Skin
Weaknesses: Fire, Flying, Rock

TYPE: BUG

POKÉMON SCARLET:
Its legs are short. Whenever it stumbles, its stiff antennae clack with a xylophone-like sound.

POKÉMON VIOLET:
When its antennae hit each other, it sounds like the music of a xylophone.

Kricketot → Kricketune

KRICKETUNE

CRICKET POKÉMON

How to Say It: KRICK-eh-toon
Imperial Height: 3'03"
Metric Height: 1.0 m
Imperial Weight: 56.2 lbs.
Metric Weight: 25.5 kg
Gender: ♂♀
Abilities: Swarm
Weaknesses: Fire, Flying, Rock

TYPE: BUG

POKÉMON SCARLET:
By allowing its cry to resonate in the hollow of its belly, it produces a captivating sound.

POKÉMON VIOLET:
There is a village that hosts a contest based on the amazingly variable cries of this Pokémon.

Kricketot Kricketune

KROKOROK

DESERT CROC POKÉMON

TYPE:
GROUND-DARK

How to Say It: KRAHK-oh-rahk
Imperial Height: 3'03"
Metric Height: 1.0 m
Imperial Weight: 73.6 lbs.
Metric Weight: 33.4 kg
Gender: ♂♀
Abilities: Intimidate, Moxie
Weaknesses: Ice, Water, Fighting, Fairy, Grass, Bug

POKÉMON SCARLET:
Protected by thin membranes, their eyes can see even in the dead of night. They live in groups of a few individuals.

POKÉMON VIOLET:
Thanks to the special membrane covering its eyes, it can see its surroundings clearly, even in the middle of the night.

Sandile → Krokorok → Krookodile

KROOKODILE

INTIMIDATION POKÉMON

How to Say It: KROOK-oh-dyle
Imperial Height: 4'11"
Metric Height: 1.5 m
Imperial Weight: 212.3 lbs.
Metric Weight: 96.3 kg
Gender: ♂♀
Abilities: Intimidate, Moxie
Weaknesses: Ice, Water, Fighting, Fairy, Grass, Bug

TYPE:
GROUND-DARK

POKÉMON SCARLET:
After clamping down with its powerful jaws, it twists its body around to rip its prey in half.

POKÉMON VIOLET:
Its unique faculty of sight can detect small prey more than 30 miles away, even in the midst of a sandstorm.

Sandile

Krokorok

Krookodile

LARVESTA

TORCH POKÉMON

How to Say It: lar-VESS-tah
Imperial Height: 3'07"
Metric Height: 1.1 m
Imperial Weight: 63.5 lbs.
Metric Weight: 28.8 kg
Gender: ♂♀
Abilities: Flame Body
Weaknesses: Water, Flying, Rock

TYPE: BUG-FIRE

POKÉMON SCARLET:

This Pokémon was called the Larva That Stole the Sun. The fire Larvesta spouts from its horns can cut right through a sheet of iron.

POKÉMON VIOLET:

In ancient times, Larvesta was worshiped as the emissary of the sun. However, it was also viewed as a burden since it often caused forest fires.

Larvesta → Volcarona

LARVITAR

ROCK SKIN POKÉMON

TYPE: ROCK-GROUND

How to Say It: LAR-vuh-tar
Imperial Height: 2'00"
Metric Height: 0.6 m
Imperial Weight: 158.7 lbs.
Metric Weight: 72.0 kg
Gender: ♂♀
Abilities: Guts
Weaknesses: Grass, Water, Fighting, Ground, Ice, Steel

POKÉMON SCARLET:

Born deep underground, this Pokémon becomes a pupa after eating enough dirt to make a mountain.

POKÉMON VIOLET:

It is born deep underground. It can't emerge until it has entirely consumed the soil around it.

Larvitar → Pupitar → Tyranitar

LEAFEON

VERDANT POKÉMON

TYPE:
GRASS

How to Say It: LEAF-ee-on
Imperial Height: 3'03"
Metric Height: 1.0 m
Imperial Weight: 56.2 lbs.
Metric Weight: 25.5 kg
Gender: ♂♀
Abilities: Leaf Guard
Weaknesses: Bug, Fire, Flying, Ice, Poison

Eevee   Leafeon

POKÉMON SCARLET:
When you see Leafeon asleep in a patch of sunshine, you'll know it is using photosynthesis to produce clean air.

POKÉMON VIOLET:
The younger they are, the more they smell like fresh grass. With age, their fragrance takes on the odor of fallen leaves.

LECHONK

HOG POKÉMON

How to Say It: leh-CHAHNK
Imperial Height: 1'08"
Metric Height: 0.5 m
Imperial Weight: 22.5 m
Metric Weight: 10.2 kg
Gender: ♂♀
Abilities: Gluttony, Aroma Veil
Weaknesses: Fighting

TYPE:
NORMAL

POKÉMON SCARLET:
It searches for food all day. It possesses a keen sense of smell but doesn't use it for anything other than foraging.

POKÉMON VIOLET:
This Pokémon spurns all but the finest of foods. Its body gives off an herblike scent that bug Pokémon detest.

Lechonk   Oinkologne

121

LILLIGANT

FLOWERING POKÉMON

How to Say It: LIL-lih-gunt
Imperial Height: 3'07"
Metric Height: 1.1 m
Imperial Weight: 35.9 lbs.
Metric Weight: 16.3 kg
Gender: ♂♀
Abilities: Chlorophyll, Own Tempo
Weaknesses: Fire, Flying, Ice, Poison, Bug

TYPE:
GRASS

POKÉMON SCARLET:

The fragrance of the garland on its head has a relaxing effect, but taking care of it is very difficult.

POKÉMON VIOLET:

No matter how much time and money is spent raising it, its flowers are the most beautiful when they bloom in the wild.

Petilil   Lilligant

LITLEO

LION CUB POKÉMON

TYPE:
FIRE-
NORMAL

How to Say It: LIT-lee-oh
Imperial Height: 2'00"
Metric Height: 0.6 m
Imperial Weight: 29.8 lbs.
Metric Weight: 13.5 kg
Gender: ♂♀
Abilities: Rivalry, Unnerve
Weaknesses: Water, Ground, Fighting, Rock

POKÉMON SCARLET:

When Litleo are young, female Pyroar will teach them how to hunt. Once the Litleo mature, they will leave the pride and set out on their own.

POKÉMON VIOLET:

The more a Litleo trains its body and spirit by battling mighty enemies, the hotter its mane will grow.

Litleo   Pyroar

LOKIX

GRASSHOPPER POKÉMON

TYPE:
BUG-DARK

How to Say It: low-kicks
Imperial Height: 3'03"
Metric Height: 1.0 m
Imperial Weight: 38.6 lbs.
Metric Weight: 17.5 kg
Gender: ♂♀
Abilities: Swarm
Weaknesses: Fire, Fairy, Flying, Bug, Rock

POKÉMON SCARLET:

When it decides to fight all out, it stands on its previously folded legs to enter Showdown Mode. It neutralizes its enemies in short order.

POKÉMON VIOLET:

It uses its normally folded third set of legs when in Showdown Mode. This places a huge burden on its body, so it can't stay in this mode for long.

Nymble → **Lokix**

LUCARIO

AURA POKÉMON

How to Say It: loo-CAR-ee-oh
Imperial Height: 3'11"
Metric Height: 1.2 m
Imperial Weight: 119.0 lbs.
Metric Weight: 54.0 kg
Gender: ♂♀
Abilities: Inner Focus, Steadfast
Weaknesses: Fighting, Fire, Ground

TYPE:
FIGHTING-
STEEL

POKÉMON SCARLET:

It's said that no foe can remain invisible to Lucario, since it can detect auras—even those of foes it could not otherwise see.

POKÉMON VIOLET:

A well-trained one can use its aura to identify and take in the feelings of creatures over half a mile away.

Riolu → Lucario

LUMINEON

NEON POKÉMON

TYPE:
WATER

How to Say It: loo-MIN-ee-on
Imperial Height: 3'11"
Metric Height: 1.2 m
Imperial Weight: 52.9 lbs.
Metric Weight: 24.0 kg
Gender: ♂♀
Abilities: Swift Swim, Storm Drain
Weaknesses: Grass, Electric

POKÉMON SCARLET:

With its shining light, it lures its prey close. However, the light also happens to attract ferocious fish Pokémon—its natural predators.

POKÉMON VIOLET:

Lumineon swimming in the darkness of the deep sea look like stars shining in the night sky.

Finneon → Lumineon

LURANTIS

BLOOM SICKLE POKÉMON

TYPE: GRASS

How to Say It: loor-RAN-tis
Imperial Height: 2'11"
Metric Height: 0.9 m
Imperial Weight: 40.8 lbs.
Metric Weight: 18.5 kg
Gender: ♂♀
Abilities: Leaf Guard
Weaknesses: Fire, Flying, Ice, Poison, Bug

POKÉMON SCARLET:
By masquerading as a bug Pokémon, it lowers the guard of actual bug Pokémon lured in by a scent of sweet flowers. Its sickles bring them down.

POKÉMON VIOLET:
A lot of time and effort is required to maintain the vivid colors of its petals. This Pokémon puts its Trainer's attentiveness to the test.

Fomantis ➡ Lurantis

LUVDISC

RENDEZVOUS POKÉMON

How to Say It: LOVE-disk
Imperial Height: 2'00"
Metric Height: 0.6 m
Imperial Weight: 19.2 lbs.
Metric Weight: 8.7 kg
Gender: ♂♀
Abilities: Swift Swim
Weaknesses: Grass, Electric

TYPE: WATER

POKÉMON SCARLET:
Its heart-shaped body makes it popular. In some places, you would give a Luvdisc to someone you love.

POKÉMON VIOLET:
During the spawning season, countless Luvdisc congregate at coral reefs, turning the waters pink.

Does not evolve.

LUXIO

SPARK POKÉMON

How to Say It: LUCKS-ee-oh
Imperial Height: 2'11"
Metric Height: 0.9 m
Imperial Weight: 67.2 lbs.
Metric Weight: 30.5 kg
Gender: ♂♀
Abilities: Intimidate, Rivalry
Weaknesses: Ground

TYPE: ELECTRIC

POKÉMON SCARLET:
Strong electricity courses through the tips of its sharp claws. A light scratch causes fainting in foes.

POKÉMON VIOLET:
By gathering their tails together, they collectively generate powerful electricity from their claws.

Shinx → Luxio → Luxray

TYPE: ELECTRIC

LUXRAY

GLEAM EYES POKÉMON

How to Say It: LUCKS-ray
Imperial Height: 4'07"
Metric Height: 1.4 m
Imperial Weight: 92.6 lbs.
Metric Weight: 42.0 kg
Gender: ♂♀
Abilities: Intimidate, Rivalry
Weaknesses: Ground

POKÉMON SCARLET:
It can see clearly through walls to track down its prey and seek its lost young.

POKÉMON VIOLET:
Luxray's ability to see through objects comes in handy when it's scouting for danger.

Shinx → Luxio → Luxray

LYCANROC

WOLF POKÉMON

POKÉMON SCARLET:
Lycanroc attacks its prey with its sharp claws and fangs. It loyally obeys the instructions of a Trainer it trusts.

POKÉMON VIOLET:
It has a calm and collected demeanor. It swiftly closes in on its prey, then slices them with the rocks in its mane.

TYPE:
ROCK

How to Say It: LIE-can-rock
Imperial Height: 2'07"
Metric Height: 0.8 m
Imperial Weight: 55.1 lbs.
Metric Weight: 25.0 kg
Gender: ♂♀
Abilities: Keen Eye, Sand Rush
Weaknesses: Water, Steel, Grass, Fighting, Ground

MIDDAY FORM

DUSK FORM

MIDNIGHT FORM

Rockruff → Lycanroc

MABOSSTIFF

BOSS POKÉMON

How to Say It: mah-BAWS-tif
Imperial Height: 3'07"
Metric Height: 1.1 m
Imperial Weight: 134.5 lbs.
Metric Weight: 61 kg
Gender: ♂♀
Abilities: Intimidate, Guard Dog
Weaknesses: Fairy, Bug, Fighting

TYPE:
DARK

POKÉMON SCARLET:

This Pokémon can store energy in its large dewlap. Mabosstiff unleashes this energy all at once to blow away enemies.

POKÉMON VIOLET:

Mabosstiff loves playing with children. Though usually gentle, it takes on an intimidating look when protecting its family.

Maschiff → Mabosstiff

MAGIKARP

FISH POKÉMON

How to Say It: MADGE-eh-karp
Imperial Height: 2'11"
Metric Height: 0.9 m
Imperial Weight: 22.0 lbs.
Metric Weight: 10.0 kg
Gender: ♂♀
Abilities: Swift Swim
Weaknesses: Electric, Grass

TYPE:
WATER

POKÉMON SCARLET:

An underpowered, pathetic Pokémon. It may jump high on rare occasions but never more than seven feet.

POKÉMON VIOLET:

In the distant past, it was somewhat stronger than the horribly weak descendants that exist today.

Magikarp Gyarados

MAGNEMITE

MAGNET POKÉMON

**TYPE:
ELECTRIC-
STEEL**

How to Say It: MAG-ne-mite
Imperial Height: 1'00"
Metric Height: 0.3 m
Imperial Weight: 13.2 lbs.
Metric Weight: 6.0 kg
Gender: Unknown
Abilities: Sturdy, Magnet Pull
Weaknesses: Fire, Fighting, Ground

POKÉMON SCARLET:

The electromagnetic waves emitted by the units at the sides of its head expel antigravity, which allows it to float.

POKÉMON VIOLET:

It moves while constantly hovering. It discharges electromagnetic waves and so on from the units at its sides.

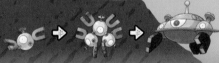

Magnemite　Magneton　Magnezone

MAGNETON

MAGNET POKÉMON

How to Say It: MAG-ne-ton
Imperial Height: 3'03"
Metric Height: 1.0 m
Imperial Weight: 132.3 lbs.
Metric Weight: 60.0 kg
Gender: Unknown
Abilities: Sturdy, Magnet Pull
Weaknesses: Fire, Fighting, Ground

**TYPE:
ELECTRIC-
STEEL**

POKÉMON SCARLET:

Three Magnemite are linked by a strong magnetic force. Earaches will occur if you get too close.

POKÉMON VIOLET:

They're formed by several Magnemite linked together. They frequently appear when sunspots flare up.

Magnemite　Magneton　Magnezone

MAGNEZONE

MAGNET AREA POKÉMON

How to Say It: MAG-nuh-zone
Imperial Height: 3'11"
Metric Height: 1.2 m
Imperial Weight: 396.8 lbs.
Metric Weight: 180.0 kg
Gender: Unknown
Abilities: Sturdy, Magnet Pull
Weaknesses: Fire, Fighting, Ground

**TYPE:
ELECTRIC-
STEEL**

POKÉMON SCARLET:

As it zooms through the sky, this Pokémon seems to be receiving signals of unknown origin while transmitting signals of unknown purpose.

POKÉMON VIOLET:

Exposure to a special magnetic field changed Magneton's molecular structure, turning it into Magnezone.

Magnemite   Magneton   Magnezone

MAKUHITA

GUTS POKÉMON

**TYPE:
FIGHTING**

How to Say It: MAK-oo-HEE-ta
Imperial Height: 3'03"
Metric Height: 1.0 m
Imperial Weight: 190.5 lbs.
Metric Weight: 86.4 kg
Gender: ♂♀
Abilities: Guts, Thick Fat
Weaknesses: Psychic, Flying, Fairy

POKÉMON SCARLET:

It grows stronger by enduring harsh training. It is a gutsy Pokémon that can withstand any attack.

POKÉMON VIOLET:

It toughens up by slamming into thick trees over and over. It gains a sturdy body and dauntless spirit.

Makuhita   Hariyama

MANKEY

PIG MONKEY POKÉMON

How to Say It: MANG-key
Imperial Height: 1'08"
Metric Height: 0.5 m
Imperial Weight: 61.7 lbs.
Metric Weight: 28.0 kg
Gender: ♂♀
Abilities: Vital Spirit, Anger Point
Weaknesses: Psychic, Flying, Fairy

POKÉMON SCARLET:

It lives in groups in the treetops. If it loses sight of its group, it becomes infuriated by its loneliness.

POKÉMON VIOLET:

It is extremely quick to anger. It could be docile one moment, then thrashing away the next instant.

Mankey → **Primeape**

MAREANIE

BRUTAL STAR POKÉMON

TYPE:

POISON-
WATER

How to Say It: muh-REE-nee
Imperial Height: 1'04"
Metric Height: 0.4 m
Imperial Weight: 17.6 lbs.
Metric Weight: 8.0 kg
Gender: ♂♀
Abilities: Limber, Merciless
Weaknesses: Psychic, Electric, Ground

POKÉMON SCARLET:

This Pokémon wanders the seaside looking for food. It often gets electric shocks from broken Pincurchin spines that it tries to eat.

POKÉMON VIOLET:

It has excellent regenerative capabilities. Legs that a Mareanie has lost have a very bitter, astringent flavor—they're not suitable as food.

Mareanie → **Toxapex**

131

MAREEP

WOOL POKÉMON

How to Say It: mah-REEP
Imperial Height: 2'00"
Metric Height: 0.6 m
Imperial Weight: 17.2 lbs.
Metric Weight: 7.8 kg
Gender: ♂♀
Abilities: Static
Weaknesses: Ground

**TYPE:
ELECTRIC**

POKÉMON SCARLET:

If static electricity builds in its body, its fleece doubles in volume. Touching it will shock you.

POKÉMON VIOLET:

Its fleece grows continually. In the summer, the fleece is fully shed, but it grows back in a week.

Mareep   Flaaffy   Ampharos

MARILL

AQUA MOUSE POKÉMON

**TYPE:
WATER-
FAIRY**

How to Say It: MARE-rull
Imperial Height: 1'04"
Metric Height: 0.4 m
Imperial Weight: 18.7 lbs.
Metric Weight: 8.5 kg
Gender: ♂♀
Abilities: Thick Fat,
Huge Power
Weaknesses: Grass,
Electric, Poison

POKÉMON SCARLET:

The fur on its body naturally repels water. It can stay dry even when it plays in the water.

POKÉMON VIOLET:

The oil-filled tail functions as a buoy, so it's fine even in rivers with strong currents.

Azurill   Marill   Azumarill

MASCHIFF

TYPE: DARK

RASCAL POKÉMON

How to Say it: MAS-sheff
Imperial Height: 1'08"
Metric Height: 0.5 m
Imperial Weight: 35.3 lbs.
Metric Weight: 16 kg
Gender: ♂♀
Abilities: Run Away, Intimidate
Weaknesses: Fairy, Bug, Fighting

Maschiff → Mabosstiff

POKÉMON SCARLET:

It always scowls in an attempt to make opponents take it seriously, but even crying children will burst into laughter when they see Maschiff's face.

POKÉMON VIOLET:

Its well-developed jaw and fangs are strong enough to crunch through boulders, and its thick fat makes for an excellent defense.

MASQUERAIN

EYEBALL POKÉMON

TYPE: BUG-FLYING

How to Say It: mas-ker-RAIN
Imperial Height: 2'07"
Metric Height: 0.8 m
Imperial Weight: 7.9 lbs.
Metric Weight: 3.6 kg
Gender: ♂♀
Abilities: Intimidate
Weaknesses: Fire, Flying, Electric, Ice, Rock

POKÉMON SCARLET:

It flaps its four wings to hover and fly freely in any direction—to and fro and sideways.

POKÉMON VIOLET:

The antennae have distinctive patterns that look like eyes. When it rains, they grow heavy, making flight impossible.

Surskit → Masquerain

133

MAUSHOLD

FAMILY POKÉMON

How to Say It: MOUSE-hold
Imperial Height: 1'00"
Metric Height: 0.3 m
Imperial Weight: 6.2 lbs.
Metric Weight: 2.3 kg
Gender: Unknown
Abilities: Cheek Pouch, Friend Guard
Weaknesses: Fighting

TYPE: **NORMAL**

POKÉMON SCARLET:

The two little ones just appeared one day. The group might be a family of related Pokémon, but nobody knows for sure.

POKÉMON VIOLET:

The larger pair protects the little ones during battles. When facing strong opponents, the whole group will join the fight.

Tandemaus → Maushold

MEDICHAM

MEDITATE POKÉMON

How to Say It: MED-uh-cham
Imperial Height: 4'03"
Metric Height: 1.3 m
Imperial Weight: 69.4 lbs.
Metric Weight: 31.5 kg
Gender: ♂♀
Abilities: Pure Power
Weaknesses: Ghost, Fairy, Flying

TYPE: **FIGHTING-PSYCHIC**

POKÉMON SCARLET:

Through yoga training, it gained the psychic power to predict its foe's next move.

POKÉMON VIOLET:

It elegantly avoids attacks with dance-like steps, then launches a devastating blow in the same motion.

Meditite → Medicham

MEDITITE

MEDITATE POKÉMON

How to Say It: MED-uh-tite
Imperial Height: 2'00"
Metric Height: 0.6 m
Imperial Weight: 24.7 lbs.
Metric Weight: 11.2 kg
Gender: ♂♀
Abilities: Pure Power
Weaknesses: Ghost, Fairy, Flying

TYPE: FIGHTING-PSYCHIC

POKÉMON SCARLET:
It never skips its daily yoga training. It heightens its inner strength through meditation.

POKÉMON VIOLET:
It meditates to heighten its inner energy and to float in the air. It eats one berry a day.

Meditite → Medicham

MEOWSCARADA

MAGICIAN POKÉMON

How to Say It: MEOW-skah-RAH-da
Imperial Height: 4'11"
Metric Height: 1.5 m
Imperial Weight: 68.8 lbs.
Metric Weight: 31.2 kg
Gender: ♂♀
Abilities: Overgrow
Weaknesses: Ice, Fire, Flying, Poison, Fighting, Fairy, Bug

TYPE: GRASS-DARK

POKÉMON SCARLET:
This Pokémon uses the reflective fur lining its cape to camouflage the stem of its flower, creating the illusion that the flower is floating.

POKÉMON VIOLET:
With skillful misdirection, it rigs foes with pollen-packed flower bombs. Meowscarada sets off the bombs before its foes realize what's going on.

Sprigatito → Floragato → Meowscarada

MEOWTH

SCRATCH CAT POKÉMON

How to Say It: mee-OWTH
Imperial Height: 1'04"
Metric Height: 0.4 m
Imperial Weight: 9.3 lbs.
Metric Weight: 4.2 kg
Gender: ♂♀
Abilities: Pickup, Technician
Weaknesses: Fighting

TYPE: NORMAL

POKÉMON SCARLET:

All it does is sleep during the daytime. At night, it patrols its territory with its eyes aglow.

POKÉMON VIOLET:

It loves things that sparkle. When it sees a shiny object, the gold coin on its head shines, too.

Meowth → Persian

MIMIKYU

DISGUISE POKÉMON

How to Say It: MEE-mee-kyoo
Imperial Height: 0'08"
Metric Height: 0.2 m
Imperial Weight: 1.5 lbs.
Metric Weight: 0.7 kg
Gender: ♂♀
Abilities: Disguise
Weaknesses: Ghost, Steel

TYPE: GHOST-FAIRY

POKÉMON SCARLET:

This Pokémon lives in dark places untouched by sunlight. When it appears before humans, it hides itself under a cloth that resembles a Pikachu.

POKÉMON VIOLET:

Mimikyu was only recently identified as a Pokémon. Previously, people thought it was just a ghost wearing a cloth.

Does not evolve.

MIRAIDON

PARADOX POKÉMON

TYPE:
ELECTRIC-DRAGON

How to Say It: meer-RAI-dahn
Imperial Height: 11'06"
Metric Height: 3.5 m
Imperial Weight: 529.1 lbs.
Metric Weight: 240.0 kg
Gender: Unknown
Abilities: Hadron Engine
Weaknesses: Fairy, Ground, Ice, Dragon

POKÉMON SCARLET:

Much remains unknown about this creature. It resembles Cyclizar, but it is far more ruthless and powerful.

POKÉMON VIOLET:

This seems to be the Iron Serpent mentioned in an old book. The Iron Serpent is said to have turned the land to ash with its lightning.

Does not evolve.

MISDREAVUS

SCREECH POKÉMON

How to Say It: mis-DREE-vuss
Imperial Height: 2'04"
Metric Height: 0.7 m
Imperial Weight: 2.2 lbs.
Metric Weight: 1.0 kg
Gender: ♂♀
Abilities: Levitate
Weaknesses: Ghost, Dark

TYPE:
GHOST

POKÉMON SCARLET:

This Pokémon startles people in the middle of the night. It gathers fear as its energy.

POKÉMON VIOLET:

It loves to bite and yank people's hair from behind without warning, just to see their shocked reactions.

Misdreavus   **Mismagius**

MISMAGIUS

MAGICAL POKÉMON

Misdreavus   **Mismagius**

How to Say It: miss-MAG-ee-us
Imperial Height: 2'11"
Metric Height: 0.9 m
Imperial Weight: 9.7 lbs.
Metric Weight: 4.4 kg
Gender: ♂♀
Abilities: Levitate
Weaknesses: Ghost, Dark

TYPE:
GHOST

POKÉMON SCARLET:

Its cry sounds like an incantation. It is said the cry may rarely be imbued with happiness-giving power.

POKÉMON VIOLET:

Its cries sound like incantations to torment the foe. It appears where you least expect it.

MORGREM

DEVIOUS POKÉMON

TYPE:
DARK-FAIRY

How to Say It: MOHR-grehm
Imperial Height: 2'07"
Metric Height: 0.8 m
Imperial Weight: 27.6 lbs.
Metric Weight: 12.5 kg
Gender: ♂
Abilities: Frisk, Prankster
Weaknesses: Steel, Fairy, Poison

Impidimp → **Morgrem** → **Grimmsnarl**

POKÉMON SCARLET:

Morgrem prefers dirty tactics, like ambushing, because it doesn't have confidence in its brawn.

POKÉMON VIOLET:

This Pokémon absorbs negative emotions and turns them into energy. It's popular with people who tend to think gloomy thoughts.

MUDBRAY

DONKEY POKÉMON

How to Say It: MUD-bray
Imperial Height: 3'03"
Metric Height: 1.0 m
Imperial Weight: 242.5 lbs.
Metric Weight: 110.0 kg
Gender: ♂♀
Abilities: Own Tempo, Stamina
Weaknesses: Water, Grass, Ice

TYPE:
GROUND

POKÉMON SCARLET:

This Pokémon covers itself in mud that it has regurgitated. The mud won't dry out even if it's exposed to the sun for a long time.

POKÉMON VIOLET:

Though a slow walker, Mudbray is plenty strong. Its pace doesn't change even when it's loaded with 50 times its own body weight.

Mudbray → **Mudsdale**

139

MUDSDALE

DRAFT HORSE POKÉMON

How to Say It: MUDZ-dale
Imperial Height: 8'02"
Metric Height: 2.5 m
Imperial Weight: 2,028.3 lbs.
Metric Weight: 920.0 kg
Gender: ♂♀
Abilities: Own Tempo, Stamina
Weaknesses: Water, Grass, Ice

TYPE: GROUND

POKÉMON SCARLET:

This Pokémon has been treasured not just for its physical labor but also because it produces high-quality mud used for making pottery.

POKÉMON VIOLET:

Its legs are fortified with mud and harder than stone, and they can reduce a large truck to scrap with one kick.

Mudbray → Mudsdale

TYPE: POISON

MUK

SLUDGE POKÉMON

How to Say It: MUCK
Imperial Height: 3'11"
Metric Height: 1.2 m
Imperial Weight: 66.1 lbs.
Metric Weight: 30.0 kg
Gender: ♂♀
Abilities: Stench, Sticky Hold
Weaknesses: Psychic, Ground

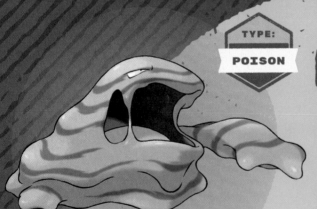

POKÉMON SCARLET:

It's thickly covered with a filthy, vile sludge. It is so toxic even its footprints contain poison.

POKÉMON VIOLET:

It's so stinky! Muk's body contains toxic elements, and any plant will wilt when it passes by.

Grimer → Muk

MURKROW

TYPE:
DARK-FLYING

How to Say It: MUR-crow
Imperial Height: 1'08"
Metric Height: 0.5 m
Imperial Weight: 4.6 lbs.
Metric Weight: 2.1 kg
Gender: ♂ ♀
Abilities: Insomnia, Super Luck
Weaknesses: Fairy, Electric, Ice, Rock

POKÉMON SCARLET:
Feared and loathed by many, it is believed to bring misfortune to all those who see it at night.

POKÉMON VIOLET:
If spotted, it will lure an unwary person into chasing it, then lose the pursuer on mountain trails.

Murkrow → Honchkrow

NACLI

ROCK SALT POKÉMON

How to Say It: NAK-lee
Imperial Height: 1'04"
Metric Height: 0.4 m
Imperial Weight: 35.3 lbs.
Metric Weight: 16.0 kg
Gender: ♂ ♀
Abilities: Sturdy, Purifying Salt
Weaknesses: Water, Steel, Grass, Fighting, Ground

TYPE:
ROCK

POKÉMON SCARLET:
It was born in a layer of rock salt deep under the earth. This species was particularly treasured in the old days, as they would share precious salt.

POKÉMON VIOLET:
The ground scrapes its body as it travels, causing it to leave salt behind. Salt is constantly being created and replenished inside Nacli's body.

Nacli → Naclstack → Garganacl

NACLSTACK

How to Say It: NAK-ull-stak
Imperial Height: 2'00"
Metric Height: 0.6 m
Imperial Weight: 231.5 lbs.
Metric Weight: 105.0 kg
Gender: ♂♀
Abilities: Sturdy, Purifying Salt
Weaknesses: Water, Steel, Grass, Fighting, Ground

TYPE: ROCK

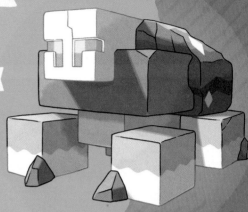

POKÉMON SCARLET:

This Pokémon dry cures its prey by spraying salt over them. The curing process steals away the water in the prey's body.

POKÉMON VIOLET:

It compresses rock salt inside its body and shoots out hardened salt pellets with enough force to perforate an iron sheet.

Nacli → Naclstack → Garganacl

NOIBAT

How to Say It: NOY-bat
Imperial Height: 1'08"
Metric Height: 0.5 m
Imperial Weight: 17.6
Metric Weight: 8.0 kg
Gender: ♂♀
Abilities: Frisk, Infiltrator
Weaknesses: Ice, Rock, Fairy, Dragon

TYPE: FLYING-DRAGON

POKÉMON SCARLET:

This Pokémon emits ultrasonic waves from its large ears to search for fruit to eat. It mistakes Applin for its food.

POKÉMON VIOLET:

Noibat can change the frequency of its sound waves at will, and it generates ultrasonic waves of up to 200,000 hertz.

Noibat → Noivern

TYPE:
FLYING-DRAGON

NOIVERN

SOUND WAVE POKÉMON

How to Say It: NOY-vurn
Imperial Height: 4'11"
Metric Height: 1.5 m
Imperial Weight: 187.4 lbs.
Metric Weight: 85.0 kg
Gender: ♂♀
Abilities: Frisk, Infiltrator
Weaknesses: Fairy, Dragon, Ice, Rock

POKÉMON SCARLET:

Ultrasonic waves emitted by a Noivern can pulverize a large boulder. This Pokémon has a cruel disposition.

POKÉMON VIOLET:

In the dark, even Hydreigon are terrified of this Pokémon. But in the light, Noivern is the one that avoids battle.

Noibat → Noivern

NUMEL

NUMB POKÉMON

How to Say It: NUM-mull
Imperial Height: 2'04"
Metric Height: 0.7 m
Imperial Weight: 52.9 lbs.
Metric Weight: 24.0 kg
Gender: ♂♀
Abilities: Oblivious, Simple
Weaknesses: Water, Ground

TYPE:
FIRE-GROUND

POKÉMON SCARLET:

Magma of almost 2,200 degrees Fahrenheit courses through its body. When it grows cold, the magma hardens and slows it.

POKÉMON VIOLET:

The flaming magma it stores in the hump on its back is the source of its tremendous power.

Numel → Camerupt

NYMBLE

GRASSHOPPER POKÉMON

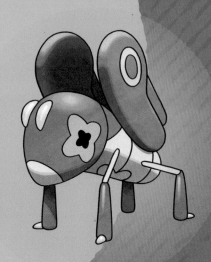

How to Say It: NIHM-bull
Imperial Height: 0'08"
Metric Height: 0.2 m
Imperial Weight: 2.2 lbs.
Metric Weight: 1.0 kg
Gender: ♂♀
Abilities: Swarm
Weaknesses: Fire, Flying, Rock

TYPE:
BUG

POKÉMON SCARLET:

It has its third set of legs folded up. When it's in a tough spot, this Pokémon jumps over 30 feet using the strength of its legs.

POKÉMON VIOLET:

It's highly skilled at a fighting style in which it uses its jumping capabilities to dodge incoming attacks while also dealing damage to opponents.

Nymble → Lokix

OINKOLOGNE

HOG POKÉMON

MALE

FEMALE

TYPE:
NORMAL

How to Say It: OIN-koh-lohn
Imperial Height: 3'03"
Metric Height: 1.0 m
Imperial Weight: 264.6 lbs.
Metric Weight: 120.0 kg
Gender: ♂♀
Abilities: Gluttony, Lingering Aroma
Weaknesses: Fighting

POKÉMON SCARLET:

Oinkologne is proud of its fine, glossy skin. It emits a concentrated scent from the tip of its tail.

POKÉMON VIOLET:

It entrances female Pokémon with the sweet, alluring scent that wafts from all over its body.

Lechonk → Oinkologne

ORANGURU

SAGE POKÉMON

How to Say It: or-RANG-goo-roo
Imperial Height: 4'11"
Metric Height: 1.5 m
Imperial Weight: 167.6 lbs.
Metric Weight: 76.0 kg
Gender: ♂♀
Abilities: Inner Focus, Telepathy
Weaknesses: Dark, Bug

TYPE:
NORMAL-PSYCHIC

POKÉMON SCARLET:

People used to mistake Oranguru for a human when they saw it issue command after command to the other Pokémon of the forest.

POKÉMON VIOLET:

This Pokémon lives quietly in the depths of the forest. The purple, cape-like fur gets longer and longer as Oranguru ages.

Does not evolve.

ORICORIO (BAILE STYLE)

DANCING POKÉMON

How to Say It: or-ih-KOR-ee-oh
Imperial Height: 2'00"
Metric Height: 0.6 m
Imperial Weight: 7.5 lbs.
Metric Weight: 3.4 kg
Gender: ♂♀
Abilities: Dancer
Weaknesses: Water, Electric, Rock

**TYPE:
FIRE-
FLYING**

POKÉMON SCARLET:

This Pokémon is incredibly popular, possibly because its passionate dancing is a great match with the temperament of Paldean people.

POKÉMON VIOLET:

This form of Oricorio has sipped red nectar. It whips up blazing flames as it moves to the steps of its passionate dance.

Does not evolve.

ORICORIO (PA'U STYLE)

DANCING POKÉMON

**TYPE:
PSYCHIC-
FLYING**

How to Say It: or-ih-KOR-ee-oh
Imperial Height: 2'00"
Metric Height: 0.6 m
Imperial Weight: 7.5 lbs.
Metric Weight: 3.4 kg
Gender: ♂♀
Abilities: Dancer
Weaknesses: Ghost, Dark, Electric, Ice, Rock

POKÉMON SCARLET:

The airy dance of these Oricorio is popular as a means of maintaining good health, but the Oricorio themselves are hard to find in Paldea.

POKÉMON VIOLET:

This form of Oricorio has sipped pink nectar. It elevates its mind with the gentle steps of its dance, then unleashes its psychic energy.

Does not evolve.

ORICORIO (POM-POM STYLE)

DANCING POKÉMON

How to Say It: or-ih-KOR-ee-oh
Imperial Height: 2'00"
Metric Height: 0.6 m
Imperial Weight: 7.5 lbs.
Metric Weight: 3.4 kg
Gender: ♂♀
Abilities: Dancer
Weaknesses: Ice, Rock

**TYPE:
ELECTRIC-
FLYING**

POKÉMON SCARLET:
This form of Oricorio has sipped yellow nectar. It uses nimble steps to approach opponents, then knocks them out with electric punches.

POKÉMON VIOLET:
The energetic, cheerful dance of these Oricorio is popular with children, but the Oricorio themselves are hard to find in Paldea.

Does not evolve.

ORICORIO (SENSU STYLE)

DANCING POKÉMON

How to Say It: or-ih-KOR-ee-oh
Imperial Height: 2'00"
Metric Height: 0.6 m
Imperial Weight: 7.5 lbs.
Metric Weight: 3.4 kg
Gender: ♂♀
Abilities: Dancer
Weaknesses: Ghost, Dark, Electric, Ice, Rock

**TYPE:
GHOST-
FLYING**

POKÉMON SCARLET:
This form of Oricorio has sipped purple nectar. It uses ethereal dance steps to call forth the spirits of the dead.

POKÉMON VIOLET:
The elegant, attractive dance of these Oricorio is popular with adults, but the Oricorio themselves are hard to find in Paldea.

Does not evolve.

ORTHWORM

EARTHWORM POKÉMON

How to Say It: ORTH-werm
Imperial Height: 8'02"
Metric Height: 2.5 m
Imperial Weight: 683.4 lbs.
Metric Weight: 310.0 kg
Gender: ♂ ♀
Abilities: Earth Eater
Weaknesses: Fire, Fighting, Ground

TYPE:
STEEL

POKÉMON SCARLET:

When attacked, this Pokémon will wield the tendrils on its body like fists and pelt the opponent with a storm of punches.

POKÉMON VIOLET:

This Pokémon lives in arid deserts. It maintains its metal body by consuming iron from the soil.

Does not evolve.

PACHIRISU

ELESQUIRREL POKÉMON

How to Say It: patch-ee-REE-sue
Imperial Height: 1'04"
Metric Height: 0.4 m
Imperial Weight: 8.6 lbs.
Metric Weight: 3.9 kg
Gender: ♂ ♀
Abilities: Run Away, Pickup
Weaknesses: Ground

TYPE:
ELECTRIC

POKÉMON SCARLET:

It's one of the kinds of Pokémon with electric cheek pouches. It shoots charges from its tail.

POKÉMON VIOLET:

A pair may be seen rubbing their cheek pouches together in an effort to share stored electricity.

Does not evolve.

PALAFIN

DOLPHIN POKÉMON

How to Say It: PAL-uh-fin
Imperial Height: 4'03"
Metric Height: 1.3 m
Imperial Weight: 132.7 lbs.
Metric Weight: 60.2 kg
Gender: ♂♀
Abilities: Zero to Hero
Weaknesses: Grass, Electric

TYPE:

WATER

POKÉMON SCARLET:

This Pokémon changes its appearance if it hears its allies calling for help. Palafin will never show anybody its moment of transformation.

POKÉMON VIOLET:

Its physical capabilities are no different than a Finizen's, but when its allies are in danger, it transforms and powers itself up.

ZERO FORM

HERO FORM

Finizen Palafin

PALOSSAND

SAND CASTLE POKÉMON

TYPE:
GHOST-GROUND

How to Say It: PAL-uh-sand
Imperial Height: 4'03"
Metric Height: 1.3 m
Imperial Weight: 551.2 lbs.
Metric Weight: 250.0 kg
Gender: ♂♀
Abilities: Water Compaction
Weaknesses: Ghost, Dark, Grass, Water, Ice

POKÉMON SCARLET:

The terrifying Palossand drags smaller Pokémon into its sandy body. Once its victims are trapped, it drains them of their vitality whenever it pleases.

POKÉMON VIOLET:

From the hollows in its arms, it fires the bones of its victims, which are all dried up after being drained of their vitality.

 →

Sandygast　　**Palossand**

PASSIMIAN

TEAMWORK POKÉMON

TYPE:
FIGHTING

How to Say It: pass-SIM-ee-uhn
Imperial Height: 6'07"
Metric Height: 2.0 m
Imperial Weight: 182.5 lbs.
Metric Weight: 82.8 kg
Gender: ♂♀
Abilities: Receiver
Weaknesses: Psychic, Flying, Fairy

POKÉMON SCARLET:

This Pokémon battles by throwing hard berries. It won't obey a Trainer who throws Poké Balls without skill.

POKÉMON VIOLET:

The boss chooses 10 members of the group to go out hunting. The hunting party will evenly split the food they find with the rest of the group.

Does not evolve.

PAWMI

MOUSE POKÉMON

TYPE: ELECTRIC

How to Say It: PAW-mi
Imperial Height: 1'00"
Metric Height: 0.3 m
Imperial Weight: 5.5 lbs.
Metric Weight: 2.5 kg
Gender: ♂♀
Abilities: Static, Natural Cure
Weaknesses: Ground

POKÉMON SCARLET:

It has underdeveloped electric sacs on its cheeks. These sacs can produce electricity only if Pawmi rubs them furiously with the pads on its forepaws.

POKÉMON VIOLET:

The pads of its paws are electricity-discharging organs. Pawmi fires electricity from its forepaws while standing unsteadily on its hind legs.

Pawmi → Pawmo → Pawmot

PAWMO

MOUSE POKÉMON

TYPE: ELECTRIC-FIGHTING

How to Say It: PAW-moh
Imperial Height: 1'04"
Metric Height: 0.4 m
Imperial Weight: 14.3 lbs.
Metric Weight: 6.5 kg
Gender: ♂♀
Abilities: Natural Cure, Volt Absorb
Weaknesses: Psychic, Fairy, Ground

POKÉMON SCARLET:

When its group is attacked, Pawmo is the first to leap into battle, defeating enemies with a fighting technique that utilizes electric shocks.

POKÉMON VIOLET:

Pawmo uses a unique fighting technique in which it uses its forepaws to strike foes and zap them with electricity from its paw pads simultaneously.

Pawmi → Pawmo → Pawmot

PAWMOT

HANDS-ON POKÉMON

How to Say It: PAW-met
Imperial Height: 2'11"
Metric Height: 0.9 m
Imperial Weight: 90.4 lbs.
Metric Weight: 41.0 kg
Gender: ♂ ♀
Abilities: Natural Cure, Volt Absorb
Weaknesses: Psychic, Fairy, Ground

TYPE:
ELECTRIC-FIGHTING

POKÉMON SCARLET:

This Pokémon normally is slow to react, but once it enters battle, it will strike down its enemies with lightning-fast movements.

POKÉMON VIOLET:

Pawmot's fluffy fur acts as a battery. It can store the same amount of electricity as an electric car.

Pawmi → Pawmo → Pawmot

PAWNIARD

Pawniard → Bisharp → Kingambit

TYPE:
DARK-STEEL

SHARP BLADE POKÉMON

How to Say It: PAWN-yard
Imperial Height: 1'08"
Metric Height: 0.5 m
Imperial Weight: 22.5 lbs.
Metric Weight: 10.2 kg
Gender: ♂♀
Abilities: Defiant, Inner Focus
Weaknesses: Fighting, Fire, Ground

POKÉMON SCARLET:

Pawniard will fearlessly challenge even powerful foes. In a pinch, it will cling to opponents and pierce them with the blades all over its body.

POKÉMON VIOLET:

Any chips in its blades would prove fatal for it. After each battle, it diligently maintains its blades using its favorite sharpening stone.

PELIPPER

WATER BIRD POKÉMON

How to Say It: PEL-pi-purr
Imperial Height: 3'11"
Metric Height: 1.2 m
Imperial Weight: 61.7 lbs.
Metric Weight: 28.0 kg
Gender: ♂♀
Abilities: Keen Eye, Drizzle
Weaknesses: Electric, Rock

TYPE:
WATER-FLYING

POKÉMON SCARLET:

It is a flying transporter that carries small Pokémon in its beak. It bobs on the waves to rest its wings.

POKÉMON VIOLET:

It protects its young in its beak. It bobs on waves, resting on them on days when the waters are calm.

Wingull → Pelipper

PERSIAN

CLASSY CAT POKÉMON

TYPE: NORMAL

How to Say It: PER-zhun
Imperial Height: 3'03"
Metric Height: 1.0 m
Imperial Weight: 70.5 lbs.
Metric Weight: 32.0 kg
Gender: ♂♀
Abilities: Limber, Technician
Weaknesses: Fighting

POKÉMON SCARLET:

Although its fur has many admirers, it is tough to raise as a pet because of its fickle meanness.

POKÉMON VIOLET:

It has a vicious temperament. Beware if it raises its tail straight up. This is a signal that it is about to pounce and bite.

Meowth → Persian

PETILIL

BULB POKÉMON

TYPE: GRASS

How to Say It: PEH-tuh-LIL
Imperial Height: 1'08"
Metric Height: 0.5 m
Imperial Weight: 14.6 lbs.
Metric Weight: 6.6 kg
Gender: ♀
Abilities: Chlorophyll, Own Tempo
Weaknesses: Fire, Flying, Ice, Poison, Bug

POKÉMON SCARLET:

The leaves on its head grow right back even if they fall out. These bitter leaves refresh those who eat them.

POKÉMON VIOLET:

If the leaves on its head are pruned with regularity, this Pokémon can be grown into a fine plump shape.

Petilil → Lilligant

PHANPY

LONG NOSE POKÉMON

TYPE: GROUND

How to Say It: FAN-pee
Imperial Height: 1'08"
Metric Height: 0.5 m
Imperial Weight: 73.9 lbs.
Metric Weight: 33.5 kg
Gender: ♂♀
Abilities: Pickup
Weaknesses: Water, Grass, Ice

POKÉMON SCARLET:

This Pokémon lives and nests on a riverbank. After playing in the mud, it won't be able to settle down unless it washes its body.

POKÉMON VIOLET:

It is far stronger than it appears. If a Phanpy is swinging its trunk around and your arm gets hit by it, your arm bone will shatter.

Phanpy → **Donphan**

PICHU

TINY MOUSE POKÉMON

How to Say It: PEE-choo
Imperial Height: 1'00"
Metric Height: 0.3 m
Imperial Weight: 4.4 lbs.
Metric Weight: 2.0 kg
Gender: ♂♀
Abilities: Pichu
Weaknesses: Ground

TYPE: ELECTRIC

POKÉMON SCARLET:

It is unskilled at storing electric power. Any kind of shock causes it to discharge energy spontaneously.

POKÉMON VIOLET:

Despite this Pokémon's cute appearance, those who want to live with one should prepare to be on the receiving end of its electric jolts.

Pichu → **Pikachu** → **Raichu**

PIKACHU

MOUSE POKÉMON

How to Say It: PEE-ka-choo
Imperial Height: 1'04"
Metric Height: 0.4 m
Imperial Weight: 13.2 lbs.
Metric Weight: 6.0 kg
Gender: ♂♀
Abilities: Static
Weaknesses: Ground

TYPE: ELECTRIC

POKÉMON SCARLET:

When it is angered, it immediately discharges the energy stored in the pouches in its cheeks.

POKÉMON VIOLET:

When several of these Pokémon gather, their electricity can build and cause lightning storms.

Pichu　　Pikachu　　Raichu

PINCURCHIN

SEA URCHIN POKÉMON

How to Say It: PIN-kur-chin
Imperial Height: 1'00"
Metric Height: 0.3 m
Imperial Weight: 2.2 lbs.
Metric Weight: 1.0 kg
Gender: ♂♀
Abilities: Lightning Rod
Weaknesses: Ground

TYPE: ELECTRIC

POKÉMON SCARLET:

This Pokémon generates electricity when it digests food. It uses its five hard teeth to scrape seaweed off surfaces and eat it.

POKÉMON VIOLET:

This Pokémon is so timid that even brushing against seaweed will make it discharge electricity in surprise. Its lips do not conduct electricity.

Does not evolve.

PINECO

BAGWORM POKÉMON

TYPE:
BUG

How to Say It: PINE-co
Imperial Height: 2'00"
Metric Height: 0.6 m
Imperial Weight: 15.9 lbs.
Metric Weight: 7.2 kg
Gender: ♂ ♀
Abilities: Sturdy
Weaknesses: Fire, Flying, Rock

POKÉMON SCARLET:

It likes to make its shell thicker by adding layers of tree bark. The additional weight doesn't bother it.

POKÉMON VIOLET:

It spits out a fluid that it uses to glue tree bark to its body. The fluid hardens when it touches air.

Pineco → Forretress

POLTEAGEIST

BLACK TEA POKÉMON

TYPE:
GHOST

How to Say It: POHL-tee-guyst
Imperial Height: 0'08"
Metric Height: 0.2 m
Imperial Weight: 0.9 lbs.
Metric Weight: 0.4 kg
Gender: Unknown
Abilities: Weak Armor
Weaknesses: Ghost, Dark

POKÉMON SCARLET:

The tea that composes Polteageist's body has a distinct and enjoyable flavor. Drinking too much, however, can be fatal.

POKÉMON VIOLET:

These Pokémon multiply by creeping into teapots and pouring themselves into leftover tea.

Sinistea → Polteageist

PRIMEAPE

PIG MONKEY POKÉMON

How to Say It: PRIME-ape
Imperial Height: 3'03"
Metric Height: 1.0 m
Imperial Weight: 70.5 lbs.
Metric Weight: 32.0 kg
Gender: ♂♀
Abilities: Vital Spirit, Anger Point
Weaknesses: Psychic, Flying, Fairy

TYPE: FIGHTING

POKÉMON SCARLET:
It becomes wildly furious if it even senses someone looking at it. It chases anyone that meets its glare.

POKÉMON VIOLET:
Some researchers theorize that Primeape remains angry even when inside a Poké Ball.

Mankey → Primeape

PSYDUCK

DUCK POKÉMON

TYPE: WATER

How to Say It: SY-duck
Imperial Height: 2'07"
Metric Height: 0.8 m
Imperial Weight: 43.2 lbs.
Metric Weight: 19.6 kg
Gender: ♂♀
Abilities: Damp, Cloud Nine
Weaknesses: Grass, Electric

POKÉMON SCARLET:
It is constantly wracked by a headache. When the headache turns intense, it begins using mysterious powers.

POKÉMON VIOLET:
If its chronic headache peaks, it may exhibit odd powers. It seems unable to recall such an episode.

Psyduck → Golduck

PUPITAR

HARD SHELL POKÉMON

**TYPE:
ROCK-
GROUND**

How to Say It: PUE-puh-tar
Imperial Height: 3'11"
Metric Height: 1.2 m
Imperial Weight: 335.1 lbs.
Metric Weight: 152.0 kg
Gender: ♂♀
Abilities: Shed Skin
Weaknesses: Grass, Water, Fighting, Ground, Ice, Steel

POKÉMON SCARLET:

This pupa flies around wildly by venting with great force the gas pressurized inside its body.

POKÉMON VIOLET:

Its shell is as hard as bedrock, and it is also very strong. Its thrashing can topple a mountain.

Larvitar → **Pupitar** → **Tyranitar**

PYROAR

ROYAL POKÉMON

How to Say It: PIE-roar
Imperial Height: 4'11"
Metric Height: 1.5 m
Imperial Weight: 179.7 lbs.
Metric Weight: 81.5 kg
Gender: ♂♀
Abilities: Rivalry, Unnerve
Weaknesses: Water, Ground, Fighting, Rock

**TYPE:
FIRE-
NORMAL**

POKÉMON SCARLET:

The females of a pride work together to bring down prey. It's thanks to them that their pride doesn't starve.

POKÉMON VIOLET:

The mane of a male Pyroar heats up to over 3,600 degrees Fahrenheit during battle. Merely approaching it will cause severe burns.

MALE

FEMALE

Litleo → **Pyroar**

QUAQUAVAL

DANCER POKÉMON

How to Say It: KWACK-wuh-vul
Imperial Height: 5'11"
Metric Height: 1.8 m
Imperial Weight: 136.5 lbs.
Metric Weight: 61.9 kg
Gender: ♂♀
Abilities: Torrent
Weaknesses: Fairy, Grass, Flying, Psychic, Electric

TYPE:
WATER-FIGHTING

POKÉMON SCARLET:

A single kick from a Quaquaval can send a truck rolling. This Pokémon uses its powerful legs to perform striking dances from far-off lands.

POKÉMON VIOLET:

Dancing in ways that evoke far-away places, this Pokémon mesmerizes all that see it. Flourishes of its decorative water feathers slice into its foes.

Quaxly → Quaxwell → Quaquaval

QUAXLY

DUCKLING POKÉMON

TYPE:
WATER

How to Say It: KWACKS-lee
Imperial Height: 1'08"
Metric Height: 0.5 m
Imperial Weight: 13.4 lbs.
Metric Weight: 6.1 kg
Gender: ♂♀
Abilities: Torrent
Weaknesses: Grass, Electric

POKÉMON SCARLET:

This Pokémon migrated to Paldea from distant lands long ago. The gel secreted by its feathers repels water and grime.

POKÉMON VIOLET:

Its strong legs let it easily swim around in even fast-flowing rivers. It likes to keep things tidy and is prone to overthinking things.

Quaxly → Quaxwell → Quaquaval

QUAXWELL

PRACTICING POKÉMON

TYPE:
WATER

How to Say It: KWACKS-well
Imperial Height: 3'11"
Metric Height: 1.2 m
Imperial Weight: 47.4 lbs.
Metric Weight: 21.5 kg
Gender: ♂ ♀
Abilities: Torrent
Weaknesses: Grass, Electric

POKÉMON SCARLET:

These Pokémon constantly run through shallow waters to train their legs, then compete with each other to see which of them kicks most gracefully.

POKÉMON VIOLET:

The hardworking Quaxwell observes people and Pokémon from various regions and incorporates their movements into its own dance routines.

Quaxly → Quaxwell → Quaquaval

QWILFISH

BALLOON POKÉMON

How to Say It: KWILL-fish
Imperial Height: 1'08"
Metric Height: 0.5 m
Imperial Weight: 8.6 lbs.
Metric Weight: 3.9 kg
Gender: ♂ ♀
Abilities: Poison Point, Swift Swim
Weaknesses: Psychic, Electric, Ground

TYPE:
WATER-
POISON

POKÉMON SCARLET:

Be cautious if this Pokémon starts sucking in water—it will soon attack by scattering the toxic spikes that grow all over its body.

POKÉMON VIOLET:

Experienced fishers say they try to catch Qwilfish in the brief moment that these Pokémon become defenseless just after launching poisonous spikes.

Does not evolve.

RABSCA

ROLLING POKÉMON

How to Say It: RABB-skah
Imperial Height: 1'00"
Metric Height: 0.3 m
Imperial Weight: 7.7 lbs.
Metric Weight: 3.5 kg
Gender: ♂♀
Abilities: Synchronize
Weaknesses: Ghost, Fire, Flying, Dark, Rock, Bug

TYPE:
BUG-PSYCHIC

POKÉMON SCARLET:

The body that supports the ball barely moves. Therefore, it is thought that the true body of this Pokémon is actually inside the ball.

POKÉMON VIOLET:

An infant sleeps inside the ball. Rabsca rolls the ball soothingly with its legs to ensure the infant sleeps comfortably.

Rellor → Rabsca

RAICHU

MOUSE POKÉMON

TYPE:
ELECTRIC

How to Say It: RYE-choo
Imperial Height: 2'07"
Metric Height: 0.8 m
Imperial Weight: 66.1 lbs.
Metric Weight: 30.0 kg
Gender: ♂♀
Abilities: Static
Weaknesses: Ground

POKÉMON SCARLET:

Its tail discharges electricity into the ground, protecting it from getting shocked.

POKÉMON VIOLET:

If the electric pouches in its cheeks become fully charged, both ears will stand straight up.

Pichu → Pikachu → Raichu

RALTS

FEELING POKÉMON

**TYPE:
PSYCHIC-
FAIRY**

How to Say It: RALTS
Imperial Height: 1'04"
Metric Height: 0.4 m
Imperial Weight: 14.6 lbs.
Metric Weight: 6.6 kg
Gender: ♂♀
Abilities: Synchronize, Trace
Weaknesses: Ghost, Steel,
Poison

Gardevoir

Ralts → Kirlia ↗
↘

Gallade

POKÉMON SCARLET:
The horns on its head provide a strong power
that enables it to sense people's emotions.

POKÉMON VIOLET:
It is highly attuned to the emotions of people
and Pokémon. It hides if it senses hostility.

RELLOR

ROLLING POKÉMON

**TYPE:
BUG**

How to Say It: RELL-lor
Imperial Height: 0'08"
Metric Height: 0.2 m
Imperial Weight: 2.2 lbs.
Metric Weight: 1.0 kg
Gender: ♂♀
Abilities: Compound Eyes
Weaknesses: Fire, Flying, Rock

POKÉMON SCARLET:
This Pokémon creates a mud ball by mixing sand
and dirt with psychic energy. It treasures its mud
ball more than its own life.

POKÉMON VIOLET:
It rolls its mud ball around while the energy it needs
for evolution matures. Eventually the time comes
for it to evolve.

Rellor → Rabsca

REVAVROOM

MULTI-CYL POKÉMON

How to Say It: REV-uh-VROOM
Imperial Height: 5'11"
Metric Height: 1.8 m
Imperial Weight: 264.6 lbs.
Metric Weight: 120.0 kg
Gender: ♂♀
Abilities: Overcoat
Weaknesses: Fire, Ground

**TYPE:
STEEL-POISON**

POKÉMON SCARLET:

It creates a gas out of poison and minerals from rocks. It then detonates the gas in its cylinders—now numbering eight—to generate energy.

POKÉMON VIOLET:

Revavroom viciously threatens others with the sound of its exhaust. It sticks its tongue out from its cylindrical mouth and sprays toxic fluids.

Varoom → Revavroom

RIOLU

EMANATION POKÉMON

How to Say It: ree-OH-loo
Imperial Height: 2'04"
Metric Height: 0.7 m
Imperial Weight: 44.5 lbs.
Metric Weight: 20.2 kg
Gender: ♂♀
Abilities: Inner Focus, Steadfast
Weaknesses: Flying, Psychic, Fairy

**TYPE:
FIGHTING**

POKÉMON SCARLET:

They communicate with one another using their auras. They are able to run all through the night.

POKÉMON VIOLET:

It has the peculiar power of being able to see emotions, such as joy and rage, in the form of waves.

Riolu → Lucario

ROARING MOON

PARADOX POKÉMON

TYPE:
DRAGON-DARK

How to Say It: ROAR-ing moon
Imperial Height: 6'07"
Metric Height: 2.0 m
Imperial Weight: 837.8 lbs.
Metric Weight: 380.0 kg
Gender: Unknown
Abilities: Protosynthesis
Weaknesses: Fairy, Ice, Bug, Fighting, Dragon

POKÉMON SCARLET:
It is possible that this is the creature listed as Roaring Moon in an expedition journal that still holds many mysteries.

POKÉMON VIOLET:
According to an article in a dubious magazine, this Pokémon has some connection to a phenomenon that occurs in a certain region.

Does not evolve.

ROCKRUFF

PUPPY POKÉMON

How to Say It: ROCK-ruff
Imperial Height: 1'08"
Metric Height: 0.5 m
Imperial Weight: 20.3 lbs.
Metric Weight: 9.2 kg
Gender: ♂♀
Abilities: Keen Eye, Vital Spirit, Own Tempo
Weaknesses: Water, Steel, Grass, Fighting, Ground

TYPE:
ROCK

POKÉMON SCARLET:
This Pokémon is very friendly when it's young. Its disposition becomes vicious once it matures, but it never forgets the kindness of its master.

POKÉMON VIOLET:
This Pokémon travels in a pack with others until it grows up. When its mood turns sour, it starts striking the ground with the rocks on its neck.

Rockruff → Lycanroc

ROLYCOLY

COAL POKÉMON

How to Say It: ROH-lee-KOH-lee
Imperial Height: 1'00"
Metric Height: 0.3 m
Imperial Weight: 26.5 lbs.
Metric Weight: 12.0 kg
Gender: ♂♀
Abilities: Heatproof, Steam Engine
Weaknesses: Water, Steel, Grass, Fighting, Ground

POKÉMON SCARLET:

On sunny days, Rolycoly will come out onto grassy plains and roll around. Then it will eat the grass that gets tangled in its wheel-like leg.

POKÉMON VIOLET:

Chunks of the surface of this Pokémon's body that have grown old and flaked off have long been used for fuel as an alternative to coal.

TYPE:
ROCK

Rolycoly   Carkol   Coalossal

ROOKIDEE

TINY BIRD POKÉMON

TYPE:
FLYING

How to Say It: ROOK-ih-dee
Imperial Height: 0'08"
Metric Height: 0.2 m
Imperial Weight: 4.0 lbs.
Metric Weight: 1.8 kg
Gender: ♂♀
Abilities: Keen Eye, Unnerve
Weaknesses: Electric, Ice, Rock

POKÉMON SCARLET:

This Pokémon is brave and reckless. The white markings around a Rookidee's eyes intimidate fainthearted Pokémon.

POKÉMON VIOLET:

The females are fussier than the males. If another creature dirties a female Rookidee's wings, it'll peck the offender relentlessly in a burning rage.

Rookidee   Corvisquire   Corviknight

ROTOM

PLASMA POKÉMON

**TYPE:
ELECTRIC-
GHOST**

How to Say It: ROW-tom
Imperial Height: 1'00"
Metric Height: 0.3 m
Imperial Weight: 0.7 lbs.
Metric Weight: 0.3 kg
Gender: Unknown
Abilities: Levitate
Weaknesses: Ghost, Dark, Ground

POKÉMON SCARLET:
Its electricity-like body can enter some kinds of machines and take control in order to make mischief.

POKÉMON VIOLET:
Research continues on this Pokémon, which could be the power source of a unique motor.

HEAT ROTOM

WASH ROTOM

FAN ROTOM

MOW ROTOM

FROST ROTOM

Does not evolve.

RUFFLET

EAGLET POKÉMON

How to Say It: RUF-lit
Imperial Height: 1'08"
Metric Height: 0.5 m
Imperial Weight: 23.1 lbs.
Metric Weight: 10.5 kg
Gender: ♂
Abilities: Keen Eye, Sheer Force
Weaknesses: Electric, Ice, Rock

TYPE:
NORMAL-FLYING

POKÉMON SCARLET:

They pick fights indiscriminately. They grow stronger and more powerful each time they faint or are injured.

POKÉMON VIOLET:

With its sharp claws, this Pokémon pierces its prey, and then it pecks at them. Although it also consumes berries, it's a carnivore at heart.

Rufflet → **Braviary**

SABLEYE

DARKNESS POKÉMON

How to Say It: SAY-bull-eye
Imperial Height: 1'08"
Metric Height: 0.5 m
Imperial Weight: 24.3 lbs.
Metric Weight: 11.0 kg
Gender: ♂♀
Abilities: Keen Eye, Stall
Weaknesses: Fairy

TYPE:
DARK-GHOST

POKÉMON SCARLET:

It dwells in the darkness of caves. It uses its sharp claws to dig up gems to nourish itself.

POKÉMON VIOLET:

Materials from gems it has eaten float to the surface of its body and can form an infinite number of patterns among individuals.

Does not evolve.

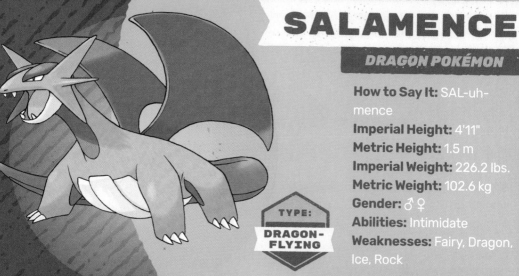

SALAMENCE

DRAGON POKÉMON

How to Say It: SAL-uh-mence

Imperial Height: 4'11"
Metric Height: 1.5 m
Imperial Weight: 226.2 lbs.
Metric Weight: 102.6 kg
Gender: ♂♀
Abilities: Intimidate
Weaknesses: Fairy, Dragon, Ice, Rock

**TYPE:
DRAGON-FLYING**

POKÉMON SCARLET:

It flies around on its wings, which have grown in at last. In its happiness, it gushes hot flames, burning up everything it passes over.

POKÉMON VIOLET:

It becomes uncontrollable if it is enraged. It destroys everything with shredding claws and fire.

Bagon → Shelgon → Salamence

SALANDIT

TOXIC LIXARD POKÉMON

How to Say It: suh-LAN-dit
Imperial Height: 2'00"
Metric Height: 0.6 m
Imperial Weight: 10.6 lbs.
Metric Weight: 4.8 kg
Gender: ♂♀
Abilities: Corrosion
Weaknesses: Water, Psychic, Ground, Rock

**TYPE:
POISON-FIRE**

POKÉMON SCARLET:

It taunts its prey and lures them into narrow, rocky areas where it then sprays them with toxic gas to make them dizzy and take them down.

POKÉMON VIOLET:

Only female Salandit can produce gas laden with pheromones. Males entranced by this gas will do whatever the females tell them.

Salandit → Salazzle

SALAZZLE

TOXIC LIZARD POKÉMON

How to Say It: suh-LAZ-zuhl
Imperial Height: 3'11"
Metric Height: 1.2 m
Imperial Weight: 48.9 lbs.
Metric Weight: 22.2 kg
Gender: ♀
Abilities: Corrosion
Weaknesses: Water, Psychic, Ground, Rock

**TYPE:
POISON-
FIRE**

POKÉMON SCARLET:

Salazzle makes its opponents light-headed with poisonous gas, then captivates them with alluring movements to turn them into loyal servants.

POKÉMON VIOLET:

When two Salazzle meet, they will use their pheromone gas to fight over the males in each other's group.

Salandit → Salazzle

SANDACONDA

SAND SNAKE POKÉMON

How to Say It: san-duh-KAHN-duh
Imperial Height: 12'06"
Metric Height: 3.8 m
Imperial Weight: 144.4 lbs.
Metric Weight: 65.5 kg
Gender: ♂ ♀
Abilities: Shed Skin, Sand Spit
Weaknesses: Water, Grass, Ice

**TYPE:
GROUND**

POKÉMON SCARLET:

It will expand its body as much as it can and then contract itself, blasting out sand with enough force to wash away a dump truck.

POKÉMON VIOLET:

The sand it spews contains sharp, pointy gravel, which is actually just sand that Sandaconda's saliva has hardened into irregular shapes.

Silicobra → Sandaconda

TYPE:
GROUND-DARK

SANDILE

DESERT CROC POKÉMON

How to Say It: SAN-dyle
Imperial Height: 2'04"
Metric Height: 0.7 m
Imperial Weight: 33.5 lbs.
Metric Weight: 15.2 kg
Gender: ♂♀
Abilities: Intimidate, Moxie
Weaknesses: Ice, Water, Fighting, Fairy, Grass, Bug

POKÉMON SCARLET:

It submerges itself in sand and moves as if swimming. This wise behavior keeps its enemies from finding it and maintains its temperature.

POKÉMON VIOLET:

They live hidden under hot desert sands in order to keep their body temperature from dropping.

Sandile → Krokorok → Krookodile

SANDY SHOCKS

PARADOX POKÉMON

How to Say It: SAN-dee shox
Imperial Height: 7'07"
Metric Height: 2.3 m
Imperial Weight: 132.3 lbs.
Metric Weight: 60.0 kg
Gender: Unknown
Abilities: Protosynthesis
Weaknesses: Water, Grass, Ice, Ground

TYPE:
ELECTRIC-GROUND

POKÉMON SCARLET:

No records exist of this Pokémon being caught. Data is lacking, but the Pokémon's traits match up with a creature shown in an expedition journal.

POKÉMON VIOLET:

It slightly resembles a Magneton that lived for 10,000 years and was featured in an article in a paranormal magazine.

Does not evolve.

SANDYGAST

SAND HEAP POKÉMON

How to Say It: SAN-dee-GAST
Imperial Height: 1'08"
Metric Height: 0.5 m
Imperial Weight: 154.3 lbs.
Metric Weight: 70.0 kg
Gender: ♂♀
Abilities: Water Compaction
Weaknesses: Ghost, Dark, Grass, Water, Ice

**TYPE:
GHOST-GROUND**

POKÉMON SCARLET:

If it loses its shovel, it will stick something else—like a branch—in its head to make do until it finds another shovel.

POKÉMON VIOLET:

It flings sand into the eyes of its prey and tries to close in on them while they're blinded, but since Sandygast is so slow, the prey tends to escape.

Sandygast → Palossand

SAWSBUCK

SEASON POKÉMON

SPRING FORM

SUMMER FORM

AUTUMN FORM

WINTER FORM

**TYPE:
NORMAL-GRASS**

How to Say It: SAWZ-buk
Imperial Height: 6'03"
Metric Height: 1.9 m
Imperial Weight: 203.9 lbs.
Metric Weight: 92.5 kg
Gender: ♂♀
Abilities: Chlorophyll, Sap Sipper
Weaknesses: Fire, Flying, Fighting, Ice, Poison, Bug

POKÉMON SCARLET:

It seems that a Sawsbuck with many flowers on its antlers will grow at a slightly slower pace because the flowers absorb the Pokémon's nutrients.

POKÉMON VIOLET:

There are many Sawsbuck enthusiasts. The paler the pink flowers that bloom on its antlers, the more beautiful the Sawsbuck is considered to be.

Deerling → Sawsbuck

172

SCATTERBUG

SCATTERDUST POKÉMON

TYPE:
BUG

How to Say It: SCAT-ter-BUG
Imperial Height: 1'00"
Metric Height: 0.3 m
Imperial Weight: 5.5 lbs.
Metric Weight: 2.5 kg
Gender: ♂♀
Abilities: Shield Dust, Compound Eyes
Weaknesses: Fire, Flying, Rock

POKÉMON SCARLET:
Any poison this Pokémon takes in is converted into a black powder and secreted. That's why Scatterbug can eat poisonous leaves and roots.

POKÉMON VIOLET:
This Pokémon scatters poisonous powder to repel enemies. It will eat different plants depending on where it lives.

Scatterbug → Spewpa → Vivillon

SCIZOR

PINCER POKÉMON

TYPE:
BUG-
STEEL

How to Say It: SIH-zor
Imperial Height: 5'11"
Metric Height: 1.8 m
Imperial Weight: 260.1 lbs.
Metric Weight: 118.0 kg
Gender: ♂♀
Abilities: Swarm, Technician
Weaknesses: Fire

POKÉMON SCARLET:
This Pokémon's pincers, which contain steel, can crush any hard object they get ahold of into bits.

POKÉMON VIOLET:
It swings its eye-patterned pincers up to scare its foes. This makes it look like it has three heads.

Scyther → Scizor

SCOVILLAIN

SPICY PEPPER POKÉMON

How to Say It: SKOH-vil-lun
Imperial Height: 2'11"
Metric Height: 0.9 m
Imperial Weight: 33.1 lbs.
Metric Weight: 15.0 kg
Gender: ♂♀
Abilities: Chlorophyll, Insomnia
Weaknesses: Flying, Poison, Rock

**TYPE:
GRASS-
FIRE**

POKÉMON SCARLET:

The red head converts spicy chemicals into fire energy and blasts the surrounding area with a super-spicy stream of flame.

POKÉMON VIOLET:

The green head has turned vicious due to the spicy chemicals stimulating its brain. Once it goes on a rampage, there is no stopping it.

Capsakid → Scovillain

SCREAM TAIL

PARADOX POKÉMON

**TYPE:
FAIRY-
PSYCHIC**

How to Say It: SCREAM tail
Imperial Height: 3'11"
Metric Height: 1.2 m
Imperial Weight: 17.6 lbs.
Metric Weight: 8.0 kg
Gender: Unknown
Abilities: Protosynthesis
Weaknesses: Steel, Ghost, Poison

POKÉMON SCARLET:

There has been only one reported sighting of this Pokémon. It resembles a mysterious creature depicted in an old expedition journal.

POKÉMON VIOLET:

It resembles a mysterious Pokémon described in a paranormal magazine as a Jigglypuff from one billion years ago.

Does not evolve.

SCYTHER

MANTIS POKÉMON

TYPE:
BUG-FLYING

How to Say It: SY-thur
Imperial Height: 4'11"
Metric Height: 1.5 m
Imperial Weight: 123.5 lbs.
Metric Weight: 56.0 kg
Gender: ♂ ♀
Abilities: Swarm, Technician
Weaknesses: Fire, Flying, Electric, Ice, Rock

POKÉMON SCARLET:
It slashes through grass with its sharp scythes, moving too fast for the human eye to track.

POKÉMON VIOLET:
The sharp scythes on its forearms become increasingly sharp by cutting through hard objects.

Scyther → Scizor

SEVIPER

FANG SNAKE POKÉMON

TYPE:
POISON

How to Say It: seh-VY-per
Imperial Height: 8'10"
Metric Height: 2.7 m
Imperial Weight: 115.7 lbs.
Metric Weight: 52.5 kg
Gender: ♂ ♀
Abilities: Shed Skin
Weaknesses: Psychic, Ground

POKÉMON SCARLET:
It sharpens its swordlike tail on hard rocks. It hides in tall grass and strikes unwary prey with venomous fangs.

POKÉMON VIOLET:
Constant polishing makes the edge of the blade on its tail extremely sharp. It's Zangoose's archrival.

Does not evolve.

SHELGON

ENDURANCE POKÉMON

How to Say It: SHELL-gon
Imperial Height: 3'07"
Metric Height: 1.1 m
Imperial Weight: 243.6 lbs.
Metric Weight: 110.5 kg
Gender: ♂♀
Abilities: Rock Head
Weaknesses: Fairy, Ice, Dragon

TYPE:
DRAGON

POKÉMON SCARLET:

The cells within its shell transform with explosive speed, preparing it for evolution.

POKÉMON VIOLET:

Its armored body makes all attacks bounce off. The armor is too tough, however, making it heavy and somewhat sluggish.

Bagon → **Shelgon** → **Salamence**

SHELLDER

BIVALVE POKÉMON

TYPE:
WATER

How to Say It: SHELL-der
Imperial Height: 1'00"
Metric Height: 0.3 m
Imperial Weight: 8.8 lbs.
Metric Weight: 4.0 kg
Gender: ♂♀
Abilities: Shell Armor, Skill Link
Weaknesses: Grass, Electric

POKÉMON SCARLET:

It is encased in a shell that is harder than diamond. Inside, however, it is surprisingly tender.

POKÉMON VIOLET:

Clamping on to an opponent reveals its vulnerable parts, so it uses this move only as a last resort.

Shellder → **Cloyster**

SHELLOS

SEA SLUG POKÉMON

TYPE: WATER

WEST SEA

EAST SEA

How to Say It: SHELL-loss
Imperial Height: 1'00"
Metric Height: 0.3 m
Imperial Weight: 13.9 lbs.
Metric Weight: 6.3 kg
Gender: ♂♀
Abilities: Sticky Hold, Storm Drain
Weaknesses: Grass, Electric

POKÉMON SCARLET:
It used to have a shell on its back long ago. This species is closely related to Pokémon like Shellder.

POKÉMON VIOLET:
It oozes a purple fluid to deter enemies. Apparently, there are more West Sea Shellos now than there were in the past.

Shellos → Gastrodon

SHINX

FLASH POKÉMON

TYPE: ELECTRIC

How to Say It: SHINKS
Imperial Height: 1'08"
Metric Height: 0.5 m
Imperial Weight: 20.9 lbs.
Metric Weight: 9.5 kg
Gender: ♂♀
Abilities: Intimidate, Rivalry
Weaknesses: Ground

POKÉMON SCARLET:
The extension and contraction of its muscles generates electricity. It glows when in trouble.

POKÉMON VIOLET:
The extension and contraction of its muscles generates electricity. Its fur glows when it's in trouble.

Shinx → Luxio → Luxray

SHROODLE

TOXIC MOUSE POKÉMON

How to Say It: SHROO-dul
Imperial Height: 0'08"
Metric Height: 0.2 m
Imperial Weight: 1.5 lbs.
Metric Weight: 0.7 kg
Gender: ♂♀
Abilities: Unburden, Pickpocket
Weaknesses: Psychic, Ground

TYPE:
POISON-NORMAL

POKÉMON SCARLET:

Though usually a mellow Pokémon, it will sink its sharp, poison-soaked front teeth into any that anger it, causing paralysis in the object of its ire.

POKÉMON VIOLET:

To keep enemies away from its territory, it paints markings around its nest using a poisonous liquid that has an acrid odor.

Shroodle   Grafaiai

SHROOMISH

MUSHROOM POKÉMON

TYPE:
GRASS

How to Say It: SHROOM-ish
Imperial Height: 1'04"
Metric Height: 0.4 m
Imperial Weight: 9.9 lbs.
Metric Weight: 4.5 kg
Gender: ♂♀
Abilities: Effect Spore, Poison Heal
Weaknesses: Fire, Flying, Ice, Poison, Bug

POKÉMON SCARLET:

It prefers damp places. By day it remains still in the forest shade. It releases toxic powder from its head.

POKÉMON VIOLET:

If it senses danger, it scatters spores from the top of its head to protect itself.

Shroomish   Breloom

SHUPPET

PUPPET POKÉMON

TYPE: GHOST

How to Say It: SHUP-pett
Imperial Height: 2'00"
Metric Height: 0.6 m
Imperial Weight: 5.1 lbs.
Metric Weight: 2.3 kg
Gender: ♂♀
Abilities: Insomnia, Frisk
Weaknesses: Ghost, Dark

POKÉMON SCARLET:

It loves to feed on feelings like envy and malice. Its upright horn catches the emotions of people.

POKÉMON VIOLET:

It feeds on the dark emotions of sadness and hatred, which make it grow steadily stronger.

Shuppet **Banette**

SILICOBRA

SAND SNAKE POKÉMON

How to Say It: sih-lih-KOH-bruh
Imperial Height: 7'03"
Metric Height: 2.2 m
Imperial Weight: 16.8 lbs.
Metric Weight: 7.6 kg
Gender: ♂♀
Abilities: Shed Skin, Sand Spit
Weaknesses: Water, Grass, Ice

TYPE: GROUND

POKÉMON SCARLET:

Silicobra's neck pouch, which can inflate and deflate like a balloon, gets more elastic each time Silicobra sheds its skin.

POKÉMON VIOLET:

Silicobra's large nostrils are specialized for spraying sand, so this Pokémon is not very good at telling apart different smells.

Silicobra **Sandaconda**

SINISTEA

BLACK TEA POKÉMON

How to Say It: SIH-nis-tee
Imperial Height: 0'04"
Metric Height: 0.1 m
Imperial Weight: 0.4 lbs.
Metric Weight: 0.2 kg
Gender: Unknown
Abilities: Weak Armor
Weaknesses: Ghost, Dark

TYPE:
GHOST

POKÉMON SCARLET:

The soul of someone who died alone possessed some leftover tea. This Pokémon appears in hotels and houses.

POKÉMON VIOLET:

Sinistea gets into your body when you drink it, and then it steals your vitality from within. It also tastes awful.

Sinistea   Polteageist

SKELEDIRGE

SINGER POKÉMON

TYPE:
FIRE-
GHOST

How to Say It: SKEL-uh-durj
Imperial Height: 5'03"
Metric Height: 1.6 m
Imperial Weight: 719.8 lbs.
Metric Weight: 326.5 kg
Gender: ♂ ♀
Abilities: Blaze
Weaknesses: Water, Ghost, Ground, Dark, Rock

POKÉMON SCARLET:

The fiery bird changes shape when Skeledirge sings. Rumor has it that the bird was born when the fireball on Skeledirge's head gained a soul.

POKÉMON VIOLET:

Skeledirge's gentle singing soothes the souls of all that hear it. It burns its enemies to a crisp with flames of over 5,400 degrees Fahrenheit.

Fuecoco   Crocalor   Skeledirge

SKIDDO

MOUNT POKÉMON

TYPE: GRASS

How to Say It: skid-OO
Imperial Height: 2'11"
Metric Height: 0.9 m
Imperial Weight: 68.3 lbs.
Metric Weight: 31.0 kg
Gender: ♂♀
Abilities: Sap Sipper
Weaknesses: Fire, Flying, Ice, Poison, Bug

POKÉMON SCARLET:
Until recently, people living in the mountains would ride on the backs of these Pokémon to traverse the mountain paths.

POKÉMON VIOLET:
As long as it has sunlight and water, Skiddo can make energy with the leaves on its body, allowing it to live on rocky mountains barren of food.

Skiddo → Gogoat

SKIPLOOM

COTTONWEED POKÉMON

How to Say It: SKIP-loom
Imperial Height: 2'00"
Metric Height: 0.6 m
Imperial Weight: 2.2 lbs.
Metric Weight: 1.0 kg
Gender: ♂♀
Abilities: Chlorophyll, Leaf Guard
Weaknesses: Fire, Flying, Ice, Poison, Rock

TYPE: GRASS-FLYING

POKÉMON SCARLET:
Skiploom enthusiasts can apparently tell where a Skiploom was born by the scent drifting from the flower on the Pokémon's head.

POKÉMON VIOLET:
When the weather grows cold, Skiploom's flower closes and the Pokémon cannot photosynthesize, so it flies away to warmer regions.

Hoppip → Skiploom → Jumpluff

SKRELP

MOCK KELP POKÉMON

How to Say It: SKRELP
Imperial Height: 1'08"
Metric Height: 0.5 m
Imperial Weight: 16.1 lbs.
Metric Weight: 7.3 kg
Gender: ♂♀
Abilities: Poison Point, Poison Touch
Weaknesses: Poison, Electric, Ground

TYPE:
POISON-WATER

POKÉMON SCARLET:

Skrelp evades its enemies by hiding amid drifting seaweed. It eats rotten seaweed to create its poison.

POKÉMON VIOLET:

This Pokémon is a poor swimmer. If it's caught in a fierce storm, it will sometimes get washed far away and become unable to return to its home.

Skrelp   **Dragalge**

SKUNTANK

SKUNK POKÉMON

How to Say It: SKUN-tank
Imperial Height: 3'03"
Metric Height: 1.0 m
Imperial Weight: 83.8 lbs.
Metric Weight: 38.0 kg
Gender: ♂♀
Abilities: Stench, Aftermath
Weaknesses: Ground

TYPE:
POISON-DARK

POKÉMON SCARLET:

It attacks by spraying a horribly smelly fluid from the tip of its tail. Attacks from above confound it.

POKÉMON VIOLET:

It attacks by spraying a repugnant fluid from its tail, but the stench dulls after a few squirts.

Stunky   **Skuntank**

SKWOVET

CHEEKY POKÉMON

TYPE: NORMAL

How to Say It: SKWUH-vet
Imperial Height: 1'00"
Metric Height: 0.3 m
Imperial Weight: 5.5 lbs.
Metric Weight: 2.5 kg
Gender: ♂♀
Abilities: Cheek Pouch
Weaknesses: Fighting

POKÉMON SCARLET:
It stores berries in its cheeks. When there are no berries to be found, Skwovet will stuff pebbles into its cheeks to stave off its cravings.

POKÉMON VIOLET:
No matter how much it stuffs its belly with food, it is always anxious about getting hungry again. So, it stashes berries in its cheeks and tail.

Skwovet → Greedent

SLAKING

LAZY POKÉMON

TYPE: NORMAL

How to Say It: SLACK-ing
Imperial Height: 6'07"
Metric Height: 2.0 m
Imperial Weight: 287.7 lbs.
Metric Weight: 130.5 kg
Gender: ♂♀
Abilities: Truant
Weaknesses: Fighting

POKÉMON SCARLET:
It is the world's most slothful Pokémon. However, it can exert horrifying power by releasing pent-up energy all at once.

POKÉMON VIOLET:
This Pokémon lives lying on its side. It only rolls over and moves when there is no more grass to eat.

Slakoth → Vigoroth → Slaking

SLAKOTH

SLACKER POKÉMON

How to Say It: SLACK-oth
Imperial Height: 2'07"
Metric Height: 0.8 m
Imperial Weight: 52.9 lbs.
Metric Weight: 24.0 kg
Gender: ♂♀
Abilities: Truant
Weaknesses: Fighting

TYPE:
NORMAL

POKÉMON SCARLET:
It sleeps for 20 hours every day. Making drowsy those that see it is one of its abilities.

POKÉMON VIOLET:
The way Slakoth lolls around makes anyone who watches it feel like doing the same.

Slakoth → Vigoroth → Slaking

SLIGGOO

SOFT TISSUE POKÉMON

TYPE:
DRAGON

How to Say It: SLIH-goo
Imperial Height: 2'07"
Metric Height: 0.8 m
Imperial Weight: 38.6 lbs.
Metric Weight: 17.5 kg
Gender: ♂♀
Abilities: Hydration, Sap Sipper
Weaknesses: Fairy, Ice, Dragon

POKÉMON SCARLET:
The swirly protrusion on its back is filled with all its vital organs, such as its brain and heart.

POKÉMON VIOLET:
When Sliggoo senses danger, the mucus coating its entire body becomes more concentrated—it'll dissolve anything.

Goomy → Sliggoo → Goodra

SLITHER WING

TYPE:
BUG-FIGHTING

How to Say It: SLIH-ther wing
Imperial Height: 10'06"
Metric Height: 3.2 m
Imperial Weight: 202.8 lbs.
Metric Weight: 92.0 kg
Gender: Unknown
Abilities: Protosynthesis
Weaknesses: Fire, Psychic, Flying, Fairy

POKÉMON SCARLET:
This mysterious Pokémon has some similarities to a creature that an old book introduced as Slither Wing.

POKÉMON VIOLET:
This Pokémon somewhat resembles an ancient form of Volcarona that was introduced in a dubious magazine.

Does not evolve.

SLOWBRO

HERMIT CRAB POKÉMON

How to Say It: SLOW-bro
Imperial Height: 5'03"
Metric Height: 1.6 m
Imperial Weight: 173.1 lbs.
Metric Weight: 78.5 kg
Gender: ♂♀
Abilities: Oblivious, Own Tempo
Weaknesses: Ghost, Dark, Grass, Electric, Bug

TYPE:
WATER-PSYCHIC

POKÉMON SCARLET:
When a Slowpoke went hunting in the sea, its tail was bitten by a Shellder. That made it evolve into Slowbro.

POKÉMON VIOLET:
If the tail-biting Shellder is thrown off in a harsh battle, this Pokémon reverts to being an ordinary Slowpoke.

Slowpoke

Slowbro

SLOWKING

ROYAL POKÉMON

How to Say It: SLOW-king
Imperial Height: 6'07"
Metric Height: 2.0 m
Imperial Weight: 175.3 lbs.
Metric Weight: 79.5 kg
Gender: ♂♀
Abilities: Oblivious, Own Tempo
Weaknesses: Ghost, Dark, Grass, Electric, Bug

TYPE:
WATER-
PSYCHIC

POKÉMON SCARLET:
When its head was bitten, toxins entered Slowpoke's head and unlocked an extraordinary power.

POKÉMON VIOLET:
It has incredible intellect and intuition. Whatever the situation, it remains calm and collected.

Slowpoke → **Slowking**

SLOWPOKE

DOPEY POKÉMON

TYPE:
WATER-
PSYCHIC

How to Say It: SLOW-poke
Imperial Height: 3'11"
Metric Height: 1.2 m
Imperial Weight: 79.4 lbs.
Metric Weight: 36.0 kg
Gender: ♂♀
Abilities: Oblivious, Own Tempo
Weaknesses: Ghost, Dark, Grass, Electric, Bug

POKÉMON SCARLET:
It is incredibly slow and dopey. It takes five seconds for it to feel pain when under attack.

POKÉMON VIOLET:
It is always vacantly lost in thought, but no one knows what it is thinking about. It is good at fishing with its tail.

Slowpoke ↗ **Slowbro**
↘ **Slowking**

SMOLIV

OLIVE POKÉMON

TYPE:
GRASS-NORMAL

How to Say It: SMAH-liv
Imperial Height: 1'00"
Metric Height: 0.3 m
Imperial Weight: 14.3 lbs.
Metric Weight: 6.5 kg
Gender: ♂♀
Abilities: Early Bird
Weaknesses: Ice, Fire, Flying, Poison, Fighting, Bug

POKÉMON SCARLET:

It protects itself from enemies by emitting oil from the fruit on its head. This oil is bitter and astringent enough to make someone flinch.

POKÉMON VIOLET:

This Pokémon converts nutrients into oil, which it stores in the fruit on its head. It can easily go a whole week without eating or drinking.

Smoliv → Dolliv → Arboliva

SNEASEL

SHARP CLAW POKÉMON

How to Say It: SNEE-zul
Imperial Height: 2'11"
Metric Height: 0.9 m
Imperial Weight: 61.7 lbs.
Metric Weight: 28.0 kg
Gender: ♂♀
Abilities: Keen Eye, Inner Focus
Weaknesses: Steel, Fire, Fighting, Rock, Fairy, Bug

TYPE:
DARK-ICE

POKÉMON SCARLET:

This cunning Pokémon hides under the cover of darkness, waiting to attack its prey.

POKÉMON VIOLET:

This is a smart and sneaky Pokémon. A pair may work together to steal eggs by having one lure the parents away.

Sneasel → Weavile

SNOM

WORM POKÉMON

TYPE:
ICE-
BUG

How to Say It: snahm
Imperial Height: 1'00"
Metric Height: 0.3 m
Imperial Weight: 8.4 lbs.
Metric Weight: 3.8 kg
Gender: ♂♀
Abilities: Shield Dust
Weaknesses: Fire, Steel,
Flying, Rock

POKÉMON SCARLET:

It eats snow that has accumulated on the ground. It prefers soft, freshly fallen snow, so it will eat its way up a mountain, aiming for the peak.

POKÉMON VIOLET:

Within its internal organs, Snom amplifies the frigid air it gets from eating snow and then uses this amplified air to create icicle-like spikes.

Snom → **Frosmoth**

SNORUNT

SNOW HAT POKÉMON

TYPE:
ICE

How to Say It: SNOW-runt
Imperial Height: 2'04"
Metric Height: 0.7 m
Imperial Weight: 37.0 lbs.
Metric Weight: 16.8 kg
Gender: ♂♀
Abilities: Inner Focus, Ice Body
Weaknesses: Fire, Steel, Fighting, Rock

Froslass

Snorunt

Glalie

POKÉMON SCARLET:

It is said that several Snorunt gather under giant leaves and live together in harmony.

POKÉMON VIOLET:

It is said that a home visited by a Snorunt will prosper. It can withstand cold of −150 degrees Fahrenheit.

SNOVER

FROST TREE POKÉMON

How to Say It: SNOW-vur
Imperial Height: 3'03"
Metric Height: 1.0 m
Imperial Weight: 111.3 lbs.
Metric Weight: 50.5 kg
Gender: ♂♀
Abilities: Snow Warning
Weaknesses: Steel, Fire, Flying, Poison, Fighting, Rock, Bug

**TYPE:
GRASS-ICE**

POKÉMON SCARLET:

During cold seasons, it migrates to the mountain's lower reaches. It returns to the snow-covered summit in the spring.

POKÉMON VIOLET:

Seemingly curious about people, they gather around footsteps they find on snowy mountains.

Snover → **Abomasnow**

SPEWPA

SCATTERDUST POKÉMON

How to Say It: SPEW-puh
Imperial Height: 1'00"
Metric Height: 0.3 m
Imperial Weight: 18.5 lbs.
Metric Weight: 8.4 kg
Gender: ♂♀
Abilities: Shed Skin
Weaknesses: Fire, Flying, Rock

**TYPE:
BUG**

POKÉMON SCARLET:

If Rufflet attacks this Pokémon by pecking at it, it will retaliate with its sharp fur and poisonous black powder.

POKÉMON VIOLET:

Spewpa doesn't live in a fixed location. It roams where it pleases across the fields and mountains, building up the energy it needs to evolve.

 Scatterbug → **Spewpa** → **Vivillon**

SPIDOPS

TRAP POKÉMON

TYPE:
BUG

How to Say It: SPY-dops
Imperial Height: 3'03"
Metric Height: 1.0 m
Imperial Weight: 36.4 lbs.
Metric Weight: 16.5 kg
Gender: ♂♀
Abilities: Insomnia
Weaknesses: Fire, Flying, Rock

POKÉMON SCARLET:

It clings to branches and ceilings using its threads and moves without a sound. It takes out its prey before the prey even notices it.

POKÉMON VIOLET:

Spidops covers its territory in tough, sticky threads to set up traps for intruders.

Tarountula → **Spidops**

SPIRITOMB

FORBIDDEN POKÉMON

TYPE:
GHOST-DARK

How to Say It: SPIR-it-tomb
Imperial Height: 3'03"
Metric Height: 1.0 m
Imperial Weight: 238.1 lbs.
Metric Weight: 108.0 kg
Gender: ♂♀
Abilities: Pressure
Weaknesses: Fairy

POKÉMON SCARLET:

Its constant mischief and misdeeds resulted in it being bound to an Odd Keystone by a mysterious spell.

POKÉMON VIOLET:

It was formed by uniting 108 spirits. It has been bound to the Odd Keystone to keep it from doing any mischief.

Does not evolve.

SPOINK

BOUNCE POKÉMON

TYPE:
PSYCHIC

How to Say It: SPOINK
Imperial Height: 2'04"
Metric Height: 0.7 m
Imperial Weight: 67.5 lbs.
Metric Weight: 30.6 kg
Gender: ♂♀
Abilities: Own Tempo, Thick Fat
Weaknesses: Ghost, Dark, Bug

POKÉMON SCARLET:
Spoink will die if it stops bouncing. The pearl on its head amplifies its psychic powers.

POKÉMON VIOLET:
Using its tail like a spring, it keeps its heart beating by bouncing constantly. If it stops, it dies.

Spoink → Grumpig

SPRIGATITO

GRASS CAT POKÉMON

How to Say It: SPRIG-uh-TEE-toh
Imperial Height: 1'04"
Metric Height: 0.4 m
Imperial Weight: 9.0 lbs.
Metric Weight: 4.1 kg
Gender: ♂♀
Abilities: Overgrow
Weaknesses: Fire, Flying, Ice, Poison, Bug

TYPE:
GRASS

POKÉMON SCARLET:
Its fluffy fur is similar in composition to plants. This Pokémon frequently washes its face to keep it from drying out.

POKÉMON VIOLET:
The sweet scent its body gives off mesmerizes those around it. The scent grows stronger when this Pokémon is in the sun.

Sprigatito → Floragato → Meowscarada

SQUAWKABILLY

PARROT POKÉMON

How to Say It: SKWAHK-uh-BIHL-ee
Imperial Height: 2'00"
Metric Height: 0.6 m
Imperial Weight: 5.3 lbs.
Metric Weight: 2.4 kg
Gender: ♂♀
Abilities: Intimidate, Hustle
Weaknesses: Electric, Ice, Rock

TYPE:
NORMAL-
FLYING

POKÉMON SCARLET:

These Pokémon prefer to live in cities. They form flocks based on the color of their feathers, and they fight over territory.

POKÉMON VIOLET:

Green-feathered flocks hold the most sway. When they're out searching for food in the mornings and evenings, it gets very noisy.

Does not evolve.

STANTLER

BIG HORN POKÉMON

TYPE:
NORMAL

How to Say It: STAN-tler
Imperial Height: 4'07"
Metric Height: 1.4 m
Imperial Weight: 157.0 lbs.
Metric Weight: 71.2 kg
Gender: ♂♀
Abilities: Intimidate, Frisk
Weaknesses: Fighting

POKÉMON SCARLET:

This Pokémon apparently used to live in much harsher environments, and thus it once had stronger psychic powers than it does now.

POKÉMON VIOLET:

It's said that this Pokémon used to be stronger long ago when it had many enemies, and that it was even able to evolve under its own power.

Does not evolve.

STARAPTOR

TYPE: NORMAL-FLYING

How to Say It: star-RAP-tor
Imperial Height: 3'11"
Metric Height: 1.2 m
Imperial Weight: 54.9 lbs.
Metric Weight: 24.9 kg
Gender: ♂♀
Abilities: Intimidate
Weaknesses: Electric, Ice, Rock

POKÉMON SCARLET:
When Staravia evolve into Staraptor, they leave the flock to live alone. They have sturdy wings.

POKÉMON VIOLET:
It never stops attacking even if it is injured. It fusses over the shape of its comb.

Starly → Staravia → Staraptor

STARAVIA

STARLING POKÉMON

How to Say It: star-EY-vee-a
Imperial Height: 2'00"
Metric Height: 0.6 m
Imperial Weight: 34.2 lbs.
Metric Weight: 15.5 kg
Gender: ♂♀
Abilities: Intimidate
Weaknesses: Electric, Ice, Rock

TYPE: NORMAL-FLYING

POKÉMON SCARLET:
Recognizing their own weakness, they always live in a group. When alone, a Staravia cries noisily.

POKÉMON VIOLET:
They maintain huge flocks, although fierce scuffles break out between various flocks.

Starly → Staravia → Staraptor

STARLY

STARLING POKÉMON

How to Say It: STAR-lee
Imperial Height: 1'00"
Metric Height: 0.3 m
Imperial Weight: 4.4 lbs.
Metric Weight: 2.0 kg
Gender: ♂ ♀
Abilities: Keen Eye
Weaknesses: Electric, Ice, Rock

TYPE:
NORMAL-
FLYING

POKÉMON SCARLET:

They flock around mountains and fields, chasing after bug Pokémon. Their singing is noisy and annoying.

POKÉMON VIOLET:

Because they are weak individually, they form groups. However, they bicker if the group grows too big.

Starly   Staravia   Staraptor

STEENEE

FRUIT POKÉMON

How to Say It: STEE-nee
Imperial Height: 2'04"
Metric Height: 0.7 m
Imperial Weight: 18.1 lbs.
Metric Weight: 8.2 kg
Gender: ♀
Abilities: Leaf Guard, Oblivious
Weaknesses: Fire, Flying, Ice, Poison, Bug

TYPE:
GRASS

POKÉMON SCARLET:

Steenee spreads a sweet scent that makes others feel invigorated. This same scent is popular for antiperspirants.

POKÉMON VIOLET:

Steenee bounces energetically through forests. If the rind that peels off its body is pulverized, it can be used to treat stomach pains.

Bounsweet   Steenee   Tsareena

STONJOURNER

BIG ROCK POKÉMON

TYPE: ROCK

How to Say It: STONE-jer-ner
Imperial Height: 8'02"
Metric Height: 2.5 m
Imperial Weight: 1,146.4 lbs.
Metric Weight: 520.0 kg
Gender: ♂♀
Abilities: Power Spot
Weaknesses: Water, Steel, Grass, Fighting, Ground

POKÉMON SCARLET:
The elemental composition of the rocks that form its body were found to match the bedrock of a land far away from this Pokémon's habitat.

POKÉMON VIOLET:
This Pokémon spends its life gazing at the setting sun. It strides leisurely across grassy plains on legs of rock that weigh over 400 pounds each.

Does not evolve.

STUNKY

SKUNK POKÉMON

How to Say It: STUNK-ee
Imperial Height: 1'04"
Metric Height: 0.4 m
Imperial Weight: 42.3 lbs.
Metric Weight: 19.2 kg
Gender: ♂♀
Abilities: Stench, Aftermath
Weaknesses: Ground

TYPE: POISON-DARK

POKÉMON SCARLET:
It sprays a foul fluid from its rear. Its stench spreads over a mile radius, driving Pokémon away.

POKÉMON VIOLET:
The foul fluid from its rear is so revolting that it can make people feel queasy up to a mile and a quarter away.

Stunky → **Skuntank**

SUDOWOODO

IMITATION POKÉMON

How to Say It: SOO-doe-WOO-doe
Imperial Height: 3'11"
Metric Height: 1.2 m
Imperial Weight: 83.8 lbs.
Metric Weight: 38.0 kg
Gender: ♂♀
Abilities: Rock Head, Sturdy
Weaknesses: Water, Steel, Fighting, Grass, Ground

TYPE: ROCK

POKÉMON SCARLET:
Although it always pretends to be a tree, its composition appears more similar to rock than to vegetation.

POKÉMON VIOLET:
To avoid being attacked, it does nothing but mimic a tree. It hates water and flees from rain.

Bonsly → **Sudowoodo**

SUNFLORA

SUN POKÉMON

TYPE: GRASS

How to Say It: SUN-FLOR-uh
Imperial Height: 2'07"
Metric Height: 0.8 m
Imperial Weight: 18.7 lbs.
Metric Weight: 8.5 kg
Gender: ♂♀
Abilities: Chlorophyll, Solar Power
Weaknesses: Fire, Flying, Ice, Poison, Bug

POKÉMON SCARLET:
In the daytime, it rushes about in a hectic manner, but it comes to a complete stop when the sun sets.

POKÉMON VIOLET:
Since it converts sunlight into energy, it is always looking in the direction of the sun.

Sunkern → **Sunflora**

SUNKERN

SEED POKÉMON

TYPE:

GRASS

How to Say It: SUN-kurn
Imperial Height: 1'00"
Metric Height: 0.3 m
Imperial Weight: 4.0 lbs.
Metric Weight: 1.8 kg
Gender: ♂♀
Abilities: Chlorophyll, Solar Power
Weaknesses: Fire, Flying, Ice, Poison, Bug

POKÉMON SCARLET:

It suddenly falls out of the sky in the morning. Knowing it's weak, it simply feeds until it evolves.

POKÉMON VIOLET:

It is very weak. Its only means of defense is to shake its leaves desperately at its attacker.

Sunkern   Sunflora

SURSKIT

POND SKATER POKÉMON

How to Say It: SUR-skit
Imperial Height: 1'08"
Metric Height: 0.5 m
Imperial Weight: 3.7 lbs.
Metric Weight: 1.7 kg
Gender: ♂♀
Abilities: Swift Swim
Weaknesses: Flying, Electric, Rock

TYPE:

BUG-WATER

POKÉMON SCARLET:

They usually live on ponds, but after an evening shower, they may appear on puddles in towns.

POKÉMON VIOLET:

It secretes a thick, sweet-scented syrup from the tip of its head. It lives on weed-choked ponds.

Surskit   Masquerain

SWABLU

COTTON BIRD POKÉMON

How to Say It: swah-BLUE
Imperial Height: 1'04"
Metric Height: 0.4 m
Imperial Weight: 2.6 lbs.
Metric Weight: 1.2 kg
Gender: ♂♀
Abilities: Natural Cure
Weaknesses: Electric, Ice, Rock

TYPE: NORMAL-FLYING

POKÉMON SCARLET:
It constantly grooms its cotton-like wings. It takes a shower to clean itself if it becomes dirty.

POKÉMON VIOLET:
It can't relax if it or its surroundings are not clean. It wipes off dirt with its wings.

Swablu → Altaria

SWALOT

POISON BAG POKÉMON

How to Say It: SWAH-lot
Imperial Height: 5'07"
Metric Height: 1.7 m
Imperial Weight: 176.4 lbs.
Metric Weight: 80.0 kg
Gender: ♂♀
Abilities: Liquid Ooze, Sticky Hold
Weaknesses: Psychic, Ground

TYPE: POISON

POKÉMON SCARLET:
It gulps anything that fits in its mouth. Its special enzymes can dissolve anything.

POKÉMON VIOLET:
It can swallow a tire whole in one gulp. It secretes a horribly toxic fluid from the pores on its body.

Gulpin → Swalot

SYLVEON

INTERTWINING POKÉMON

TYPE:
FAIRY

How to Say It: SIL-vee-on
Imperial Height: 3'03"
Metric Height: 1.0 m
Imperial Weight: 51.8 lbs.
Metric Weight: 23.5 kg
Gender: ♂♀
Abilities: Cute Charm
Weaknesses: Steel, Poison

POKÉMON SCARLET:

This Pokémon uses its ribbonlike feelers to send a soothing aura into its opponents, erasing their hostility.

POKÉMON VIOLET:

Sylveon cuts an elegant figure as it dances lightly around, feelers fluttering, but its piercing moves aim straight for its opponents' weak spots.

Eevee ➡ Sylveon

TADBULB

ELETADPOLE POKÉMON

How to Say It: TAD-bulb
Imperial Height: 1'00"
Metric Height: 0.3 m
Imperial Weight: 0.9 lbs.
Metric Weight: 0.4 kg
Gender: ♂♀
Abilities: Static, Own Tempo
Weaknesses: Ground

TYPE:
ELECTRIC

POKÉMON SCARLET:

Tadbulb shakes its tail to generate electricity. If it senses danger, it will make its head blink on and off to alert its allies.

POKÉMON VIOLET:

It floats using the electricity stored in its body. When thunderclouds are around, Tadbulb will float higher off the ground.

Tadbulb   Bellibolt

TALONFLAME

SCORCHING POKÉMON

How to Say It: TAL-un-flame
Imperial Height: 3'11"
Metric Height: 1.2 m
Imperial Weight: 54.0 lbs.
Metric Weight: 24.5 kg
Gender: ♂♀
Abilities: Flame Body
Weaknesses: Water, Electric, Rock

TYPE:
FIRE-FLYING

POKÉMON SCARLET:

It has top-notch flying capabilities. It flies around easily, even while carrying prey that weighs more than 220 lbs.

POKÉMON VIOLET:

When it gets excited, it vents sparks from the gaps between its feathers. These unburnable feathers are used as a fireproof material.

Fletchling → **Fletchinder** → **Talonflame**

TYPE:
NORMAL

TANDEMAUS

COUPLE POKÉMON

How to Say It: TAN-duh-mouse
Imperial Height: 1'00"
Metric Height: 0.3 m
Imperial Weight: 4.0 lbs.
Metric Weight: 1.8 kg
Gender: Unknown
Abilities: Run Away, Pickup
Weaknesses: Fighting

POKÉMON SCARLET:

Exhibiting great teamwork, they use their incisors to cut pieces out of any material that might be useful for a nest, then make off with them.

POKÉMON VIOLET:

The pair sticks together no matter what. They split any food they find exactly in half and then eat it together.

Tandemaus → **Maushold**

TAROUNTULA

STRING BALL POKÉMON

TYPE:
BUG

How to Say It: tuh-ROWN-chuh-luh
Imperial Height: 1'00"
Metric Height: 0.3 m
Imperial Weight: 8.8 lbs.
Metric Weight: 4.0 kg
Gender: ♂♀
Abilities: Insomnia
Weaknesses: Fire, Flying, Rock

POKÉMON SCARLET:

The ball of threads wrapped around its body is elastic enough to deflect the scythes of Scyther, this Pokémon's natural enemy.

POKÉMON VIOLET:

The thread it secretes from its rear is as strong as wire. The secret behind the thread's strength is the topic of ongoing research.

Tarountula → Spidops

TATSUGIRI

MIMICRY POKÉMON

How to Say It: TAHT-soo-gee-ree
Imperial Height: 1'00"
Metric Height: 0.3 m
Imperial Weight: 17.6 lbs.
Metric Weight: 8.0 kg
Gender: ♂♀
Abilities: Commander
Weaknesses: Fairy, Dragon

TYPE:
DRAGON-WATER

CURLY FORM

DROOPY FORM

STRETCHY FORM

POKÉMON SCARLET:

This is a small dragon Pokémon. It lives inside the mouth of Dondozo to protect itself from enemies on the outside.

POKÉMON VIOLET:

Tatsugiri is an extremely cunning Pokémon. It feigns weakness to lure in prey, then orders its partner to attack.

Does not evolve.

PALDEAN

TAUROS (AQUA BREED)

WILD BULL POKÉMON

How to Say It: TORE-ros
Imperial Height: 4'07"
Metric Height: 1.4 m
Imperial Weight: 242.5 lbs.
Metric Weight: 110.0 kg
Gender: ♂
Abilities: Intimidate, Anger Point
Weaknesses: Psychic, Flying, Grass, Fairy, Electric

TYPE:
FIGHTING-
WATER

POKÉMON SCARLET:

This Pokémon blasts water from holes on the tips of its horns—the high-pressure jets pierce right through Tauros's enemies.

POKÉMON VIOLET:

It swims by jetting water from its horns. The most notable characteristic of the Aqua Breed is its high body fat, which allows it to float easily.

Does not evolve.

PALDEAN

TAUROS (BLAZE BREED)

WILD BULL POKÉMON

TYPE:
FIGHTING-FIRE

How to Say It: TORE-ros
Imperial Height: 4'07"
Metric Height: 1.4 m
Imperial Weight: 187.4 lbs.
Metric Weight: 85.0 kg
Gender: ♂
Abilities: Intimidate, Anger Point
Weaknesses: Water, Psychic, Flying, Ground

POKÉMON SCARLET:

When heated by fire energy, its horns can get hotter than 1,800 degrees Fahrenheit. Those gored by them will suffer both wounds and burns.

POKÉMON VIOLET:

People call this kind of Tauros the Blaze Breed due to the hot air it snorts from its nostrils. Its three tails are intertwined.

Does not evolve.

PALDEAN

TAUROS (COMBAT BREED)

WILD BULL POKÉMON

How to Say It: TORE-ros
Imperial Height: 4'07"
Metric Height: 1.4 m
Imperial Weight: 253.5 lbs.
Metric Weight: 115.0 kg
Gender: ♂
Abilities: Intimidate, Anger Point
Weaknesses: Psychic, Flying, Fairy

TYPE:
FIGHTING

POKÉMON SCARLET:

This Pokémon has a muscular body and excels at close-quarters combat. It uses its short horns to strike the opponent's weak spots.

POKÉMON VIOLET:

This kind of Tauros, known as the Combat Breed, is distinguished by its thick, powerful muscles and its fierce disposition.

Does not evolve.

TEDDIURSA

LITTLE BEAR POKÉMON

How to Say It: TED-dee-UR-sa
Imperial Height: 2'00"
Metric Height: 0.6 m
Imperial Weight: 19.4 lbs.
Metric Weight: 8.8 kg
Gender: ♂♀
Abilities: Pickup, Quick Feet
Weaknesses: Fighting

TYPE: NORMAL

POKÉMON SCARLET:
This Pokémon discreetly follows Combee to find their hive. It scoops up big dollops of honey in its palms to eat.

POKÉMON VIOLET:
Its paws are soaked in oodles of honey. When nervous, Teddiursa will lick its paws and soon have a smile back on its face.

Teddiursa　→　Ursaring

LEGENDARY POKÉMON TING-LU

RUINOUS POKÉMON

How to Say It: TIHNG-loo
Imperial Height: 8'10"
Metric Height: 2.7 m
Imperial Weight: 1,542.6 lbs.
Metric Weight: 699.7 kg
Gender: Unknown
Abilities: Vessel of Ruin
Weaknesses: Fighting, Water, Ice, Fairy, Grass, Bug

TYPE: DARK-GROUND

POKÉMON SCARLET:
The fear poured into an ancient ritual vessel has clad itself in rocks and dirt to become a Pokémon.

POKÉMON VIOLET:
It slowly brings its exceedingly heavy head down upon the ground, splitting the earth open with huge fissures that run over 160 feet deep.

Does not evolve.

TINKATINK

METALSMITH POKÉMON

TYPE:
FAIRY-STEEL

How to Say It: TIHNK-uh-tihnk
Imperial Height: 1'04"
Metric Height: 0.4 m
Imperial Weight: 19.6 lbs.
Metric Weight: 8.9 kg
Gender: ♀
Abilities: Own Tempo, Mold Breaker
Weaknesses: Fire, Ground

POKÉMON SCARLET:

It swings its handmade hammer around to protect itself, but the hammer is often stolen by Pokémon that eat metal.

POKÉMON VIOLET:

This Pokémon pounds iron scraps together to make a hammer. It will remake the hammer again and again until it's satisfied with the result.

Tinkatink → Tinkatuff → Tinkaton

TINKATON

HAMMER POKÉMON

How to Say It: TIHNK-uh-tuhn
Imperial Height: 2'04"
Metric Height: 0.7 m
Imperial Weight: 248.7 lbs.
Metric Weight: 112.8 kg
Gender: ♀
Abilities: Own Tempo, Mold Breaker
Weaknesses: Fire, Ground

TYPE:
FAIRY-STEEL

POKÉMON SCARLET:

This intelligent Pokémon has a very daring disposition. It knocks rocks into the sky with its hammer, aiming for flying Corviknight.

POKÉMON VIOLET:

The hammer tops 220 pounds, yet it gets swung around easily by Tinkaton as it steals whatever it pleases and carries its plunder back home.

Tinkatink → Tinkatuff → Tinkaton

TINKATUFF

HAMMER POKÉMON

How to Say It: TIHNK-uh-tuhf
Imperial Height: 2'04"
Metric Height: 0.7 m
Imperial Weight: 130.3 lbs.
Metric Weight: 59.1 kg
Gender: ♀
Abilities: Own Tempo, Mold Breaker
Weaknesses: Fire, Ground

TYPE:
FAIRY-STEEL

POKÉMON SCARLET:

This Pokémon will attack groups of Pawniard and Bisharp, gathering metal from them in order to create a large and sturdy hammer.

POKÉMON VIOLET:

These Pokémon make their homes in piles of scrap metal. They test the strength of each other's hammers by smashing them together.

Tinkatink   Tinkatuff   Tinkaton

TOEDSCOOL

WOODEAR POKÉMON

TYPE:
GROUND-GRASS

How to Say It: TOHDS-cool
Imperial Height: 2'11"
Metric Height: 0.9 m
Imperial Weight: 72.8 lbs.
Metric Weight: 33.0 kg
Gender: ♂ ♀
Abilities: Mycelium Might
Weaknesses: Fire, Flying, Bug, Ice

POKÉMON SCARLET:

Toedscool lives in muggy forests. The flaps that fall from its body are chewy and very delicious.

POKÉMON VIOLET:

Though it looks like Tentacool, Toedscool is a completely different species. Its legs may be thin, but it can run at a speed of 30 mph.

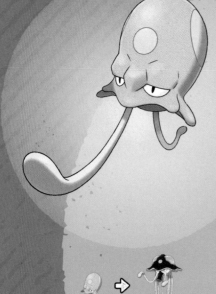

Toedscool   Toedscruel

TOEDSCRUEL

WOODEAR POKÉMON

TYPE:
GROUND-GRASS

How to Say It: TOHDS-croo-ull
Imperial Height: 6'03"
Metric Height: 1.9 m
Imperial Weight: 127.9 lbs.
Metric Weight: 58.0 kg
Gender: ♂ ♀
Abilities: Mycelium Might
Weaknesses: Fire, Flying, Bug, Ice

Toedscool → Toedscruel

POKÉMON SCARLET:
These Pokémon gather into groups and form colonies deep within forests. They absolutely hate it when strangers approach.

POKÉMON VIOLET:
It coils its 10 tentacles around prey and sucks out their nutrients, causing the prey pain. The folds along the rim of its head are a popular delicacy.

TORKOAL

COAL POKÉMON

How to Say It: TOR-coal
Imperial Height: 1'08"
Metric Height: 0.5 m
Imperial Weight: 177.3 lbs.
Metric Weight: 80.4 kg
Gender: ♂ ♀
Abilities: White Smoke, Drought
Weaknesses: Water, Ground, Rock

TYPE:
FIRE

POKÉMON SCARLET:
It burns coal inside its shell for energy. It blows out black soot if it is endangered.

POKÉMON VIOLET:
Coal is the source of Torkoal's energy. Large amounts of coal can be found in the mountains where they live.

Does not evolve.

TOXAPEX

BRUTAL STAR POKÉMON

How to Say It: TOX-uh-pex
Imperial Height: 2'04"
Metric Height: 0.7 m
Imperial Weight: 32.0 lbs.
Metric Weight: 14.5 kg
Gender: ♂♀
Abilities: Limber, Merciless
Weaknesses: Psychic, Electric, Ground

TYPE: POISON-WATER

Mareanie → Toxapex

TOXEL

BABY POKÉMON

How to Say It: TAHKS-ull
Imperial Height: 1'04"
Metric Height: 0.4 m
Imperial Weight: 24.3 lbs.
Metric Weight: 11.0 kg
Gender: ♂♀
Abilities: Static, Rattled
Weaknesses: Psychic, Ground

TYPE: ELECTRIC-POISON

Toxel → Toxtricity

TOXICROAK

TOXIC MOUTH POKÉMON

TYPE: POISON-FIGHTING

How to Say It: TOX-uh-croak
Imperial Height: 4'03"
Metric Height: 1.3 m
Imperial Weight: 97.9 lbs.
Metric Weight: 44.4 kg
Gender: ♂ ♀
Abilities: Dry Skin, Anticipation
Weaknesses: Psychic, Flying, Ground

POKÉMON SCARLET:

Swaying and dodging the attacks of its foes, it weaves its flexible body in close, then lunges out with its poisonous claws.

POKÉMON VIOLET:

It has a poison sac at its throat. When it croaks, the stored poison is churned for greater potency.

Croagunk → Toxicroak

TOXTRICITY

PUNK POKÉMON

How to Say It: tahks-TRIS-ih-tee
Imperial Height: 5'03"
Metric Height: 1.6 m
Imperial Weight: 88.2 lbs.
Metric Weight: 40.0 kg
Gender: ♂ ♀
Abilities: Minus, Punk Rock
Weaknesses: Psychic, Ground

TYPE: ELECTRIC-POISON

POKÉMON SCARLET:

Many youths admire the way this Pokémon listlessly picks fights and keeps its cool no matter what opponent it faces.

POKÉMON VIOLET:

As it gulps down stagnant water and generates electricity in its body, a sound like a rhythm played by a bass guitar reverberates all around.

AMPED FORM

LOW KEY FORM

Toxel → Toxtricity

TROPIUS

FRUIT POKÉMON

How to Say It: TROP-ee-us
Imperial Height: 6'07"
Metric Height: 2.0 m
Imperial Weight: 220.5 lbs.
Metric Weight: 100.0 kg
Gender: ♂♀
Abilities: Chlorophyll, Solar Power
Weaknesses: Fire, Flying, Ice, Poison, Rock

TYPE: GRASS-FLYING

POKÉMON SCARLET:
It lives in tropical jungles. The bunch of fruit around its neck is delicious. The fruit grows twice a year.

POKÉMON VIOLET:
Delicious fruits grew out from around its neck because it always ate the same kind of fruit.

Does not evolve.

TSAREENA

FRUIT POKÉMON

TYPE: GRASS

How to Say It: zar-EE-nuh
Imperial Height: 3'11"
Metric Height: 1.2 m
Imperial Weight: 47.2 lbs.
Metric Weight: 21.4 kg
Gender: ♀
Abilities: Leaf Guard, Queenly Majesty
Weaknesses: Fire, Flying, Ice, Poison, Bug

POKÉMON SCARLET:
This Pokémon is proud and aggressive. However, it is said that a Tsareena will instantly become calm if someone touches the crown on its calyx.

POKÉMON VIOLET:
This Pokémon launches fierce yet elegant kicks with its long, slender legs. It views Quaquaval as its rival.

Bounsweet ➡ **Steenee** ➡ **Tsareena**

TYNAMO

ELEFISH POKÉMON

TYPE:
ELECTRIC

How to Say It: TIE-nah-moh
Imperial Height: 0'08"
Metric Height: 0.2 m
Imperial Weight: 0.7 lbs.
Metric Weight: 0.3 kg
Gender: ♂♀
Abilities: Levitate
Weaknesses: Ground

POKÉMON SCARLET:

While one alone doesn't have much power, a chain of many Tynamo can be as powerful as lightning.

POKÉMON VIOLET:

These Pokémon move in schools. They have an electricity-generating organ, so they discharge electricity if in danger.

Tynamo → Eelektrik → Eelektross

TYRANITAR

ARMOR POKÉMON

How to Say It: tie-RAN-uh-tar
Imperial Height: 6'07"
Metric Height: 2.0 m
Imperial Weight: 445.3 lbs.
Metric Weight: 202.0 kg
Gender: ♂♀
Abilities: Sand Stream
Weaknesses: Steel, Fighting, Water, Fairy, Grass, Bug, Ground

TYPE:
ROCK-DARK

POKÉMON SCARLET:

Extremely strong, it can change the landscape. It is so insolent that it doesn't care about others.

POKÉMON VIOLET:

In just one of its mighty hands, it has the power to make the ground shake and mountains crumble.

Larvitar → Pupitar → Tyranitar

UMBREON

MOONLIGHT POKÉMON

How to Say It: UM-bree-on
Imperial Height: 3'03"
Metric Height: 1.0 m
Imperial Weight: 59.5 lbs.
Metric Weight: 27.0 kg
Gender: ♂♀
Abilities: Synchronize
Weaknesses: Fairy, Bug, Fighting

TYPE: DARK

POKÉMON SCARLET:
When exposed to the moon's aura, the rings on its body glow faintly and it gains a mysterious power.

POKÉMON VIOLET:
When darkness falls, the rings on the body begin to glow, striking fear in the hearts of anyone nearby.

Eevee → Umbreon

URSARING

HIBERNATOR POKÉMON

TYPE: NORMAL

How to Say It: UR-sa-ring
Imperial Height: 5'11"
Metric Height: 1.8 m
Imperial Weight: 277.3 lbs.
Metric Weight: 125.8 kg
Gender: ♂♀
Abilities: Guts, Quick Feet
Weaknesses: Fighting

POKÉMON SCARLET:
It usually wears a hardened expression, but when it's licking up honey—which it loves—the joy it feels will cause it to break into a wide grin.

POKÉMON VIOLET:
It is quite skilled at climbing trees. If it comes across a Primeape while searching for berries in the treetops, trouble will surely ensue.

Teddiursa → Ursaring

VAPOREON

BUBBLE JET POKÉMON

TYPE: WATER

How to Say It: vay-POUR-ree-on
Imperial Height: 3'03"
Metric Height: 1.0 m
Imperial Weight: 63.9 lbs.
Metric Weight: 29.0 kg
Gender: ♂ ♀
Abilities: Water Absorb
Weaknesses: Grass, Electric

POKÉMON SCARLET:
It lives close to water. Its long tail is ridged with a fin, which is often mistaken for a mermaid's.

POKÉMON VIOLET:
Its cell composition is similar to water molecules. As a result, it can't be seen when it melts away into water.

Eevee → Vaporeon

VAROOM

SINGLE-CYL POKÉMON

TYPE: STEEL-POISON

How to Say It: vuh-ROOM
Imperial Height: 3'03"
Metric Height: 1.0 m
Imperial Weight: 77.2 lbs.
Metric Weight: 35.0 kg
Gender: ♂ ♀
Abilities: Overcoat
Weaknesses: Fire, Ground

POKÉMON SCARLET:
It is said that this Pokémon was born when an unknown poison Pokémon entered and inspirited an engine left at a scrap-processing factory.

POKÉMON VIOLET:
The steel section is Varoom's actual body. This Pokémon clings to rocks and converts the minerals within into energy to fuel its activities.

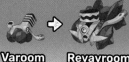

Varoom → Revavroom

VELUZA

JETTISON POKÉMON

**TYPE:
WATER-
PSYCHIC**

How to Say It: veh-LOOZ-uh
Imperial Height: 8'02"
Metric Height: 2.5 m
Imperial Weight: 198.4 lbs.
Metric Weight: 90.0 kg
Gender: ♂ ♀
Abilities: Mold Breaker
Weaknesses: Ghost, Dark, Grass, Electric, Bug

POKÉMON SCARLET:
When Veluza discards unnecessary flesh, its mind becomes honed and its psychic power increases. The spare flesh has a mild but delicious flavor.

POKÉMON VIOLET:
Veluza has excellent regenerative capabilities. It sheds spare flesh from its body to boost its agility, then charges at its prey.

Does not evolve.

**TYPE:
BUG-
POISON**

VENOMOTH

POISON MOTH POKÉMON

How to Say It: VEH-no-moth
Imperial Height: 4'11"
Metric Height: 1.5 m
Imperial Weight: 27.6 lbs.
Metric Weight: 12.5 kg
Gender: ♂ ♀
Abilities: Shield Dust, Tinted Lens
Weaknesses: Fire, Psychic, Flying, Rock

POKÉMON SCARLET:
The wings are covered with dustlike scales. Every time it flaps its wings, it looses highly toxic dust.

POKÉMON VIOLET:
When it attacks, it flaps its large wings violently to scatter its poisonous powder all around.

Venonat → Venomoth

VENONAT

INSECT POKÉMON

TYPE:
BUG-POISON

How to Say It: VEH-no-nat
Imperial Height: 3'03"
Metric Height: 1.0 m
Imperial Weight: 66.1 lbs.
Metric Weight: 30.0 kg
Gender: ♂ ♀
Abilities: Compound Eyes, Tinted Lens
Weaknesses: Fire, Psychic, Flying, Rock

POKÉMON SCARLET:
Poison oozes from all over its body. It catches small bug Pokémon at night that are attracted by light.

POKÉMON VIOLET:
Its eyes act as radar, enabling it to be active in darkness. The eyes can also shoot powerful beams.

Venonat → Venomoth

VESPIQUEN

BEEHIVE POKÉMON

How to Say It: VES-pih-kwen
Imperial Height: 3'11"
Metric Height: 1.2 m
Imperial Weight: 84.9 lbs.
Metric Weight: 38.5 kg
Gender: ♀
Abilities: Pressure
Weaknesses: Fire, Flying, Electric, Ice, Rock

TYPE:
BUG-FLYING

POKÉMON SCARLET:
It houses its colony in cells in its body and releases various pheromones to make those grubs do its bidding.

POKÉMON VIOLET:
It raises grubs in the holes in its body. It secretes pheromones to control Combee.

Combee → Vespiquen

VIGOROTH

WILD MONKEY POKÉMON

How to Say It: VIG-er-roth
Imperial Height: 4'07"
Metric Height: 1.4 m
Imperial Weight: 102.5 lbs.
Metric Weight: 46.5 kg
Gender: ♂♀
Abilities: Vital Spirit
Weaknesses: Fighting

TYPE:
NORMAL

POKÉMON SCARLET:

Its stress level rises if it cannot keep moving constantly. Too much stress makes it feel sick.

POKÉMON VIOLET:

It is always hungry because it won't stop rampaging. Even while it is eating, it can't keep still.

Slakoth **Vigoroth** **Slaking**

VIVILLON

SCALE POKÉMON

How to Say It: VIH-vee-yon
Imperial Height: 3'11"
Metric Height: 1.2 m
Imperial Weight: 37.5 lbs.
Metric Weight: 17.0 kg
Gender: ♂♀
Abilities: Shield Dust, Compound Eyes
Weaknesses: Fire, Flying, Electric, Ice, Rock

TYPE:
BUG-FLYING

POKÉMON SCARLET:

The patterns on this Pokémon depend on the climate and topography of the land it was born in. This form is from a mysterious land.

POKÉMON VIOLET:

This Pokémon was born in a mysterious land. It scatters colorful, toxic scales from its wings during battle.

Scatterbug **Spewpa** **Vivillon**

VOLCARONA

TYPE:
BUG-FIRE

How to Say It: vol-kah-ROH-nah
Imperial Height: 5'03"
Metric Height: 1.6 m
Imperial Weight: 101.4 lbs.
Metric Weight: 46.0 kg
Gender: ♂♀
Abilities: Flame Body
Weaknesses: Water, Flying, Rock

Larvesta → Volcarona

POKÉMON SCARLET:

Its burning body causes it to be unpopular in hot parts of the world, but in cold ones, Volcarona is revered as an embodiment of the sun.

POKÉMON VIOLET:

This Pokémon scatters burning scales. Most of the danger of these scales is not in their heat—it's in the way they rob the surrounding air of oxygen.

VOLTORB

BALL POKÉMON

How to Say It: VOLT-orb
Imperial Height: 1'08"
Metric Height: 0.5 m
Imperial Weight: 22.9 lbs.
Metric Weight: 10.4 kg
Gender: ♂♀
Abilities: Static, Soundproof
Weaknesses: Ground

TYPE:
ELECTRIC

POKÉMON SCARLET:

It rolls to move. If the ground is uneven, a sudden jolt from hitting a bump can cause it to explode.

POKÉMON VIOLET:

It's usually found in power plants. Easily mistaken for a Poké Ball, it has zapped many people.

Voltorb → Electrode

WATTREL

STORM PETREL POKÉMON

How to Say It: WAHT-rel
Imperial Height: 1'04"
Metric Height: 0.4 m
Imperial Weight: 7.9 lbs.
Metric Weight: 3.6 kg
Gender: ♂♀
Abilities: Volt Absorb, Wind Power
Weaknesses: Ice, Rock

TYPE:
ELECTRIC-FLYING

POKÉMON SCARLET:

When its wings catch the wind, the bones within produce electricity. This Pokémon dives into the ocean, catching prey by electrocuting them.

POKÉMON VIOLET:

These Pokémon make their nests on coastal cliffs. The nests have a strange, crackling texture, and they're a popular delicacy.

Wattrel → **Kilowattrel**

WEAVILE

SHARP CLAW POKÉMON

TYPE:
DARK-ICE

How to Say It: WEE-vile
Imperial Height: 3'07"
Metric Height: 1.1 m
Imperial Weight: 75.0 lbs.
Metric Weight: 34.0 kg
Gender: ♂♀
Abilities: Pressure
Weaknesses: Steel, Fire, Fighting, Rock, Fairy, Bug

POKÉMON SCARLET:

Evolution made it even more devious. It communicates by clawing signs in boulders.

POKÉMON VIOLET:

They travel in groups of four or five, leaving signs for one another on trees and rocks. They bring down their prey with coordinated attacks.

Sneasel → **Weavile**

WHISCASH

WHISKERS POKÉMON

TYPE: WATER-GROUND

How to Say It: WISS-cash
Imperial Height: 2'11"
Metric Height: 0.9 m
Imperial Weight: 52.0 lbs.
Metric Weight: 23.6 kg
Gender: ♂♀
Abilities: Oblivious, Anticipation
Weaknesses: Grass

POKÉMON SCARLET:
It is extremely protective of its territory. If any foe approaches, it attacks using vicious tremors.

POKÉMON VIOLET:
Sighting Whiscash leaping from the water is believed to herald an earthquake.

Barboach → **Whiscash**

WIGGLYTUFF

BALLOON POKÉMON

How to Say It: WIG-lee-tuff
Imperial Height: 3'03"
Metric Height: 1.0 m
Imperial Weight: 26.5 lbs.
Metric Weight: 12.0 kg
Gender: ♂♀
Abilities: Cute Charm, Competitive
Weaknesses: Steel, Poison

TYPE: NORMAL-FAIRY

POKÉMON SCARLET:
It has a very fine fur. Take care not to make it angry, or it may inflate steadily and hit with a body slam.

POKÉMON VIOLET:
The rich, fluffy fur that covers its body feels so good that anyone who feels it can't stop touching it.

Igglybuff → **Jigglypuff** → **Wigglytuff**

WIGLETT

GARDEN EEL POKÉMON

How to Say It: WIG-let
Imperial Height: 3'11"
Metric Height: 1.2 m
Imperial Weight: 4.0 lbs.
Metric Weight: 1.8 kg
Gender: ♂♀
Abilities: Gooey, Rattled
Weaknesses: Grass, Electric

TYPE: WATER

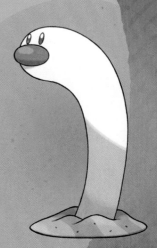

POKÉMON SCARLET:
This Pokémon can pick up the scent of a Veluza just over 65 feet away and will hide itself in the sand.

POKÉMON VIOLET:
Though it looks like Diglett, Wiglett is an entirely different species. The resemblance seems to be a coincidental result of environmental adaptation.

Wiglett → Wugtrio

WINGULL

SEAGULL POKÉMON

TYPE: WATER-FLYING

How to Say It: WING-gull
Imperial Height: 2'00"
Metric Height: 0.6 m
Imperial Weight: 20.9 lbs.
Metric Weight: 9.5 kg
Gender: ♂♀
Abilities: Keen Eye, Hydration
Weaknesses: Electric, Rock

POKÉMON SCARLET:
It soars high in the sky, riding on updrafts like a glider. It carries food tucked in its bill.

POKÉMON VIOLET:
It rides upon ocean winds as if it were a glider. In the winter, it hides food around its nest.

Wingull → Pelipper

WO-CHIEN

RUINOUS POKÉMON

TYPE:
DARK-GRASS

How to Say It: WOH-chyehn
Imperial Height: 4'11"
Metric Height: 1.5 m
Imperial Weight: 163.6 lbs.
Metric Weight: 74.2 kg
Gender: Unknown
Abilities: Tablets of Ruin
Weaknesses: Fire, Flying, Fighting, Ice, Poison, Fairy, Bug

POKÉMON SCARLET:

The grudge of a person punished for writing the king's evil deeds upon wooden tablets has clad itself in dead leaves to become a Pokémon.

POKÉMON VIOLET:

It drains the life force from vegetation, causing nearby forests to instantly wither and fields to turn barren.

Does not evolve.

PALDEAN

WOOPER

POISON FISH POKÉMON

How to Say It: WOOP-pur
Imperial Height: 1'04"
Metric Height: 0.4 m
Imperial Weight: 24.3 lbs.
Metric Weight: 11.0 kg
Gender: ♂♀
Abilities: Poison Point, Water Absorb
Weaknesses: Water, Psychic, Ice, Ground

TYPE:
POISON-GROUND

POKÉMON SCARLET:

After losing a territorial struggle, Wooper began living on land. The Pokémon changed over time, developing a poisonous film to protect its body.

POKÉMON VIOLET:

It's dangerous for Wooper to travel alone. They line up in groups of three or four and help each other as they walk around the wetlands.

Paldean Wooper

Clodsire

WUGTRIO

GARDEN EEL POKÉMON

How to Say It: WUHG-TREE-oh
Imperial Height: 3'11"
Metric Height: 1.2 m
Imperial Weight: 11.9 lbs.
Metric Weight: 5.4 kg
Gender: ♂ ♀
Abilities: Gooey, Rattled
Weaknesses: Grass, Electric

TYPE:
WATER

POKÉMON SCARLET:

It has a vicious temperament, contrary to what its appearance may suggest. It wraps its long bodies around prey, then drags the prey into its den.

POKÉMON VIOLET:

A variety of fish Pokémon, Wugtrio was once considered to be a regional form of Dugtrio.

Wiglett   Wugtrio

YUNGOOS

LOITERING POKÉMON

TYPE:
NORMAL

How to Say It: YUNG-goose
Imperial Height: 1'04"
Metric Height: 0.4 m
Imperial Weight: 13.2 lbs.
Metric Weight: 6.0 kg
Gender: ♂ ♀
Abilities: Strong Jaw, Stakeout
Weaknesses: Fighting

POKÉMON SCARLET:

Its stomach fills most of its torso. It wanders the same path every day, searching for fresh food.

POKÉMON VIOLET:

It spends its waking hours searching endlessly for food. When Yungoos is hungry, its ferocity gains a certain edge.

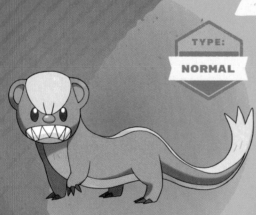

Yungoos   Gumshoos

ZANGOOSE

CAT FERRET POKÉMON

TYPE:
NORMAL

How to Say It: ZANG-goose
Imperial Height: 4'03"
Metric Height: 1.3 m
Imperial Weight: 88.8 lbs.
Metric Weight: 40.3 kg
Gender: ♂♀
Abilities: Immunity
Weaknesses: Fighting

POKÉMON SCARLET:

It's Seviper's archrival. To threaten those it encounters, it fans out the claws on its front paws.

POKÉMON VIOLET:

If it comes across a Seviper, its fur bristles and it assumes its battle pose. Its sharp claws are its best weapon.

Does not evolve.

ZOROARK

ILLUSION FOX POKÉMON

How to Say It: ZORE-oh-ark
Imperial Height: 5'03"
Metric Height: 1.6 m
Imperial Weight: 178.8 lbs.
Metric Weight: 81.1 kg
Gender: ♂♀
Abilities: Illusion
Weaknesses: Fairy, Bug, Fighting

TYPE:
DARK

POKÉMON SCARLET:

Stories say those who tried to catch Zoroark were trapped in an illusion and punished.

POKÉMON VIOLET:

Each has the ability to fool a large group of people simultaneously. They protect their lair with illusory scenery.

Zorua → **Zoroark**

ZORUA

TRICKY FOX POKÉMON

How to Say It: ZORE-oo-ah
Imperial Height: 2'04"
Metric Height: 0.7 m
Imperial Weight: 27.6 lbs.
Metric Weight: 12.5 kg
Gender: ♂♀
Abilities: Illusion
Weaknesses: Fairy, Bug, Fighting

TYPE:
DARK

POKÉMON SCARLET:

It changes into the forms of others to surprise them. Apparently, it often transforms into a silent child.

POKÉMON VIOLET:

To protect themselves from danger, they hide their true identities by transforming into people and Pokémon.

Zorua → Zoroark

ZWEILOUS

HOSTILE POKÉMON

How to Say It: ZVY-lus
Imperial Height: 4'07"
Metric Height: 1.4 m
Imperial Weight: 110.2 lbs.
Metric Weight: 50.0 kg
Gender: ♂♀
Abilities: Hustle
Weaknesses: Fairy, Fighting, Bug, Ice, Dragon

TYPE:
DARK-DRAGON

POKÉMON SCARLET:

The two heads do not get along at all. If you don't give each head the same amount of attention, they'll begin fighting out of jealousy.

POKÉMON VIOLET:

The two heads have different likes and dislikes. Because the heads fight with each other, Zweilous gets stronger without needing to rely on others.

Deino → Zweilous → Hydreigon